I0546249

HOLLY & IVY

A Dysfunctional Christmas Novella

Allison McWood

Annelid Press

Annelid Press

This book is a work of fiction. The characters, incidents and dialogue are drawn from the author's imagination and are not to be construed as real. Any resemblance to actual events or persons, living or dead, is entirely coincidental.

Holly and Ivy. Copyright © 2022 by Allison McWood. All rights reserved. No part of this book may be used or reproduced in any manner whatsoever without written permission except in the case of brief quotations embodied in critical articles and reviews. For information address Annelid Press. www.annelidpress.com.

FIRST EDITION

Cover design by Daniel Greenhalgh

ISBN: 978-1-990292-32-3

CHAPTER ONE
(ONE WEEK BEFORE CHRISTMAS)

"Memories in a bottle?" Bartrum Brower said, squinting cynically at Holly Plover.

Poised, Holly took a discreet breath, mustering boldness as she locked eyes with the stubborn executives in the room. "These products will fly off the shelves," she said confidently. She secretly hoped the executives did not notice her ankle wobble on her perfectly red stiletto. That would ruin everything.

"This is a rather ambitious notion, Ms. Plover," Gareth Port exhaled while leaning back in his leather conference chair. "A tough sell. The whole thing sounds pretty soppy and almost infantile to me."

"Some of our fondest, childhood memories involve smells," Holly explained, spritzing her wrists with perfume and urging Brower and Port to sniff. "And no childhood memories are as vivid as those associated with Christmas. I have replicated these memories and bottled them."

"What is this?" Port grimaced as he inhaled the scent on Holly's wrist. "Spruce needle?"

"Freshly cut," Holly nodded assertively. "Our new line also includes Grandma's turkey, shortbread, apple cider, hot cocoa with cinnamon, minty candy cane..."

"Chestnuts roasting on an open fire?" Brower snorted sarcastically.

"The lab is still working on that one," Holly smirked.

Brower took a long whiff of a perfume bottle he swiped from the boardroom table. "This smells like... wrapping paper and scotch tape?"

"The smell of Christmas morning," Holly explained. "Innovative, yes?"

Brower and Port glared at Holly for a moment, causing her to swallow hard. Her heart was thumping like the tail of an agitated beaver on an eerily calm lake. She stood motionless for a moment, maintaining composure and resisting the urge to fidget nervously with the back of her earring. She felt vulnerable up there at the front of the room but there was no way she would reveal that secret to her two biggest, potential clients. Her eyeballs lolled back and forth between the surly executives until she finally saw them look at one another approvingly. Holly exhaled a long breath of air she did not even realize she had been hoarding in her lungs.

"Are there more?" Brower asked, raising an inquiring eyebrow.

Holly handed a number of perfume samples to Brower and Port with a confident spring in her step. "Sentimental," she said with professional finesse. Practical. On trend. Broad commercial appeal..." Holly stopped abruptly when she saw Port wipe a tear with his silk hankie. "Mr. Port?"

"This smells like my mom's gingerbread," Port wiped a tear and honked into a handkerchief. "It's uncanny."

Holly glowed with satisfaction until she heard Brower clear his throat, which was his habit when he was about to throw a monkey wrench into one's well laid plans.

"What about eggnog?" Brower barked.

"Oh…" Holly said, stumped. She was always so well prepared. Her stomach sank and she could almost hear her confidence drain out of her body with the sound effect of a slide whistle. "I could alert the lab…"

"You claim there is a scent for everyone," Brower said, leaning in challengingly. "In my books, Christmas without eggnog is like Monday without Bourbon."

"But…" Holly hesitated. Why was she hesitating? She never hesitated. "… Christmas is only one week away."

"No nog, no deal."

Holly's mouth dropped open stupidly, but the words just dangled silently in the air. Brower was asking for the impossible. It took the lab most of the year to establish the scents they already had. There was no way they could drum up a new fragrance – incidentally a scent that had no business being sprayed on any human body part – in only seven days.

"We were under the impression we were dealing with the top perfumery in Manhattan," Port said, folding his arms in a way that Holly decided was condescending.

Holly straightened her shoulders, choosing her next words extremely carefully. "Sirs…"

"Is there a problem, Ms. Plover?"

"I..." Holly hesitated. Crap. Yes, there was a problem. A colossal problem. This was the mother of all problems, in fact. Did these guys even understand how perfume worked? Chemistry? The concept of time? Holly had never lost a deal in her life. She could not admit defeat, even in the face of pure and utter cluelessness. "Of course not," she lied. "There is no problem at all."

***

"That is going to pose a problem," Rex the chemical technician said while brisk walking alongside Holly, down a sterile hall.

"Brower and Port want the prototype by Monday so the product can make it onto the shelves before Christmas," Holly insisted.

"Monday," Rex said, counting on his fingers for dramatic effect. "That gives us like three days. And even if we were able to pull this off, that means the product wouldn't be on the shelves until at least Christmas Eve. Maybe the twenty-third if we hire a medieval alchemist. How is any of this even worth it?"

"Don't let me down, Rex."

"But the lab has been busting a hump...".

"I know, Rex."

"... for more than eleven months..."

"I realize that, Rex."

"...to launch the product we already have."

"Rex, the account is conditional on this new fragrance."

"You're talking like a crazy person, Holly. We can't do this in three days."

"This account is so important to me..."

"So is my sanity," Rex grunted.

Holly sighed assertively through her nose. She whipped her head towards Rex, causing her sleek, black, bobbed hair to swoosh dogmatically. "This is arguably the most pivotal opportunity of my career..."

"Holly..."

"Shuh-shuh-shuh," Holly shushed with a silencing index finger. "If I lose this deal it will tarnish my perfect record."

"But these Brower and Port freaks are making demands like science is some sort of witchcraft that can be brewed overnight."

"I need this, Rex."

"Why? You're already enviously successful. Have you *seen* your apartment? Your wardrobe? Your paycheck? What more do you have to prove? And to whom?"

"Losing this deal will look very bad on me, Rex. People will think I'm slipping. They will question my competence. It's the curse of being an overachiever. You have to constantly outdo yourself."

"Holly, it's Christmas though."

"Don't blow this for me, Rex."

Rex gaped at Holly as she spun defiantly around the corner.

***

There was a spring in her stride as Holly walked purposefully towards her office. Her assistant Philomena looked up from her desk which was obsessively decorated with the most kitsch Christmas ornaments imaginable. Red and green garland was stapled around the perimeter of her desk with little, felt stockings, each stuffed with last year's sticky candy canes. Plastic mistletoe was hanging shamelessly over Philomena's chair. A mismatched Nativity scene was displayed in full view consisting of a Fisher Price barn, chipped ceramic magi, (one with a missing head) cheaply plastic shepherds from the Dollar Store, a swaddled thimble with eyes, a virginal Queen Elsa and a re-purposed GI Joe figurine that barely passed as Joseph. A dancing snowman menacingly bopped around and sang the Frosty song each time someone walked by.

Philomena's dangly, jingle bell earrings tinkled as she turned to Holly with a glint in her eye.

"Holly?" Philomena practically grunted as she hauled out a huge, ornate Christmas gift basket. "This came for you."

Barely breaking her stride, Holly spun around, her eyes widening with intrigue. Briefly forgetting her meticulous professionalism, Holly rummaged girlishly through the basket. Trying painfully to suppress giddy squeals, she found champagne, chocolate dipped strawberries, imported cheese and two beautifully rectangular, perfectly perforated strips of cardboard with printed words that made Holly's eyes pop.

"Onegin tickets?" Holly basically squeaked. "The chivalrous rascal. Taking me to the ballet despite his strong opinions of ballet slippers."

Astonished to find even more goodies in this seemingly bottomless basket of fun, Holly pulled out a satin nightshirt with a pattern of cartoon feet all over it. Holly pursed her lips with silly sentimentality and hugged the shirt tightly. "Oh my god, look at this."

Philomena cocked her head.

"Feet," Holly explained. "It's an in-joke."

"You two are adorable," Philomena said with a teasing grin as she continued cutting out paper snowflakes. Her earrings tinkled even more as she playfully shook her head. She was always looking for an excuse to make her earrings tinkle.

"He is pretty great," Holly said, holding the nightshirt up in order to bask in all of its wonderfulness.

"So you've got a smoldering boyfriend," Philomena said coyly, "enviable job, cool digs, your shoes are amazing..."

"They are cute, aren't they," Holly said, modeling her shoes boastfully.

"Seriously though," Philomena teased. "If I didn't like you so much, I'd hate you. If your life was any more perfect, people would stop believing you're real."

Holly took a chocolate truffle from the gift basket and playfully tossed it at Philomena's head. "Oh stop," Holly laughed.

"Are you and Cash going to get married or what?" Philomena laughed as she dodged the truffle.

Holly's wide grin morphed into a slightly uncomfortable, pin-straight smile. "He hasn't asked."

"Oh he will," Philomena said in a singsong voice. "Sending you all these romantic gifts. Random phone calls throughout the day. Little secret notes that he doesn't think I read before passing on to you..."

"Philomena!"

"I've seen the way he looks at you, Holly. He's smitten."

Holly blushed.

"Have you even thought about it? I mean you've been all over each other for like two years and you don't even live together."

"Um, whoa. You're delving into some pretty personal subject matter, Mena."

"I'm just saying it's weird. The two of you can barely stand being apart and yet you dwell in separate residences. Can't blame a girl for making an observation."

"It's complicated. Nuanced. We both worked our tails off to buy apartments that we are in love with."

"But," Philomena said, drawing some kind if invisible diagram in the air with her fingers, "the two of you are in love with *each other.*"

"Very much so."

"Then what are you waiting for?"

Holly lugged the basket into her office, winking at Philomena. "There are some things that must remain mysterious. Else they will lose their wonder."

***

Engrossed in her work, Holly sat deathly still in her office, boring through a perfume prototype with her eyes. Her ringing phone made her grunt with frustration, but her face softened into a smile when she saw the name on the call display.

"Hey," Holly said, answering the phone. The smile on her face could literally be heard in her voice.

"Did you get it?" Cash asked, simultaneously looking at a foot scan in his podiatry office.

"Yeah, I got it," Holly said flirtatiously. "Super thoughtful. What inspired this gift? Did I feed starving orphans in a previous life?"

"Oh probably," chortled Cash. "But I sent the basket mainly because I'm sweet on Manhattan's most distinguished, perfume executive."

"Aww."

"How'd it go today?"

"They loved my presentation."

"Knew it."

"They lapped it up like a couple of thirsty whippets."

"Of course they did."

"One of them was reduced to tears."

"Wait, what?" Cash choked unexpectedly on a sudden laugh.

"Port."

"The surly one?"

"They're both surly. Port is the emotionally decrepit one with the dead eyes."

"He cried?" Cash gushed. "Awesome."

"I don't like to brag but... well, you know."

"Listen, Holls..."

"Hmmm?"

"My last patient cancelled. I could take you out to celebrate. Maybe that French place you like near Gramercy Park?"

"Oh..." Holly deflated as she goggled at the impossibly tall pile of paperwork on her desk. "I wish I could, Cash. But I'm stuck here for a bit. The lab's working on a new fragrance and we're all pulling overtime here."

"Crap. 'Til when?"

"Oh gosh, I don't know exactly. 11:30. Maybe midnight. You better eat without me."

Holly could hear a painfully long exhale coming out of a gravely disappointed version of Cash.

"You really have to stick around for that?" he asked quietly. "I had something special planned."

Holly was distracted by Rex who was standing in the doorway, gesturing towards her.

"I'll make it up to you."

"Holls…"

"Ciao," Holly said absently as she shut off her phone. She was unnerved by the quivering mouth of Rex. "Rex," Holly said, expecting the worst.

"Eggnog, Holly?" Rex spat, "Eggnog?"

"We're not having this conversation again, Rex. The deal's been made."

"Anyone who wants to bottle a dairy-based beverage and spray it on their neck should be given pills."

"If we don't keep our clients happy…"

"What you're asking us to do defies every law of chemistry."

"The nog is not negotiable."

"I could be here all night," Rex screeched.

"Crunch time, Rex. A few all-nighters never hurt anyone."

Fuming, Rex spun around to leave the room but then thought better of it. His face was red with fury like a jar of beets. "Tonight, I was supposed to take my six-year-old niece to see the Nutcracker."

Holly's lips parted. She had a feeling she was about to deservingly be sentenced to an eternity in Hell. "She'll understand," Holly said, almost inaudibly, pretending to sort papers.

"Understand?" Rex wailed. "Holly, she's six. She doesn't understand long division."

"Rex, I get that you're frustrated. There's other places I'd rather be too but…"

"The world will not come to an end if we don't kiss these wankers' butts."

"It'll be the end of my world, Rex. I've been salivating over this deal for the past…"

"You just don't get it, do you Holly?"

"What? What's that supposed to mean?"

Rex pursed his lips grudgingly. "You'd see this differently if you had a family."

Holly felt strangled by grief and remorse as she speechlessly gaped at Rex thundering out of the room.

CHAPTER TWO

Despite the ridiculously late hour the city was bustling and decked out for the holidays. Dazzling, blinking lights shone so brightly, midnight could be mistaken for noon. Late night shoppers bundled in festive scarves and bulky coats ambled down the sidewalks in droves. Dirty slush sprayed the immaculate snow each time a taxi drove by. Manhattan had no idea, nor did it care what time it was.

Holly strode in perfect sync with the city's up-tempo rhythm, wearing stylishly impractical knee-high boots with treacherously high heels. They were the perfectly red, glamorous equivalent to her saucy red stilettos. Regardless of her boots' glowering lack of functionality, Holly had mastered an elegant trot, defiantly treading on the icy street without incident.

A glowing store window, framed by flawless, sparkling garland stopped Holly in her tracks. The most perfect sweater was begging for attention on the manly chest of a mannequin behind the frosty glass. Holly let out a little gasp as she ogled the sweater through the window, like a child marveling at an array of toys in an emporium.

"Want!" Holly whimpered to herself.

The boutique door jangled, announcing Holly's arrival as she pushed open the door that was resisting with the wind. A poised clerk surveyed Holly as though she was a standard poodle in an elite dog show. Holly removed a pristine, white hat that was so immaculately fluffy, it took painful amounts of self-control for strangers not to stroke it like a live bunny rabbit. Delicate snowflakes instantly melted on her jet black, pin straight hair that had just enough body to bounce each time she took a step. The Christmas lights that gleamed through the window created a festive sheen on Holly's sleek, meticulously coiffed hair.

Gawking at the dreamy sweater and feeling the glorious material between her fingers, Holly uttered a faint whimper.

"It's imported from Italy," the poised clerk announced in a fabricated accent of what was probably a fictitious country.

"Do you have any idea how perfect this is?" Holly asked with her voice trembling like wind chimes.

"I do, actually," the clerk said smugly.

"My man is going to sizzle in this sweater."

"Would you like that in moss, camel, azure, merlot or Tuscan Sky?" the clerk asked, already assembling flat gift boxes.

Holly pondered. Cash smoldered in green. But blues brought out the oceanic perfection of his deep, blue eyes. But he looked so rugged in earth tones. And he would look strangely erotic in any color named after a wine. Holly tapped her credit card thoughtfully against the sales counter, pondering intensely. She imagined Cash in each color, squinting in concentration. While Cash looked irresistible in just about any color, there was always the slim possibility that he could have an aversion to camel. *But EARTH TONES!* And would azure draw attention to his gorgeous irises or just make him look like a blue, watery puddle? *But oh my God! Those eyes!* Then there was the question of Merlot...

"Is there some kind of a problem?" the clerk asked while twitching from the annoying, tap of Holly's credit card.

Holly could feel herself starting to sweat. Would it be possible to make a wrong decision? And if so, would it ruin Christmas? Everything just had to be perfect.

"Yes!" Holly finally blurted.

The clerk triangulated an eyebrow.

"You asked if I wanted moss, camel, azure, Merlot or Tuscan Sky. The answer is yes. I want all of them."

"All of them?" the clerk asked condescendingly as she eyeballed Holly up and down, appraising her clothing for signals of wealth.

"Money is not an issue," Holly said, wagging her credit card boastfully.

The clerk's rigid frown morphed into a prim grin as she accepted Holly's method of payment.

CHAPTER THREE

Toppling into her posh apartment with armloads of shopping bags, Holly paused for a moment when she smelled something unusual. Tantalizingly unusual. After briefly narrowing her eyes in concentration, Holly scrambled to hide all her shopping bags, realizing she was not alone in the apartment, which was tastefully and elegantly decorated for Christmas. She was startled to hear soft music playing and a romantic table set for two with delicately dripping candles, glimmering silverware and red rose petals scattered across the pristine tablecloth.

"Kitten?" Cash called from the kitchen.

Holly gasped and hastily shoved the remaining shopping bags out of sight in a linen closet as Cash sauntered in, looking dashing. His intense, blue eyes twinkled from the candle flames. His black, gelled hair boasted perfectly sleek curls. He was wearing those pants. The ones that cradled his sweet butt in a way that made Holly's insides wobble. Pulling a chair out for Holly, Cash sported one of his signature smiles with enviably white teeth. He had the best enamel. "Is seafood ravioli okay?"

"Cash," Holly beamed, "it's after midnight."

"Are you saying you already ate?" Cash asked, seating himself across from Holly.

"No but…"

"Then you're probably starving," Cash winked.

Holly nestled contentedly in her chair, looking around the apartment blissfully. This was perfect. Everything was perfect. Every Christmas decoration matched, from the uniform garland that adorned every window and mantle to the seasonal throw cushions on her ivory, leather couch. Everything glimmered in the soft, ivory lights. Not a pointsettia, candle, parcel, ornament or fiber optic snowflake was out of place.

Cash patted the chair next to his, gesturing for Holly to put her feet up for an impromptu massage. Holly winced and then made a blissful humming noise when Cash found a magical pressure point.

"Dating a podiatrist is awesome," she said dreamily.

"You've got some nasty swelling here. What did you do?"

"Whatever you're doing, it's working."

"You need to be kinder to your arches, Holls."

"My arches will forgive me if they continue getting this kind of full-service attention."

"Your shoes, Holly. They are going to murder your poor feet. I keep telling you that."

"Don't pick on my shoes. They're adorable."

Holly's cell phone had the nerve to buzz. Cash confiscated the phone before Holly had a chance to grab it.

"It's probably Rex from the lab," Holly said, pleadingly.

"You're off duty."

"Cash…"

"One, relaxing evening isn't going to make you less amazing."

Holly struggled not to relax but when Cash coyly massaged another one of his secret pressure points on Holly's foot, she went into instant relaxation mode, as though falling under the influence of hypnosis.

"Are you sure you're not God?" Holly said dreamily.

"If I was, I would never divulge my secret," Cash winked.

"Where did I find you?" Holly moaned playfully.

"On my examination table," Cash teased. "With some of the most grotesque bunions I've ever seen."

"Thank God for long hours and triangular shoes," Holly said, drowning in the depths of Cash's eyes.

The moment was perfect; candlelight flickering in Cash's eyeballs, his hair glistening with salon product, the maddening stubble on his dimpled chin, that look he gave her that said, *"Hi! You're hot and now I'm going to snog you."* Holly leaned in towards Cash with her eyelids drooping with lust, at the very moment that a kitchen timer dinged.

"One sec," Cash said, dashing from the table at the most poorly timed moment imaginable. "The pasta has achieved an ideal texture. Can't leave it in the water too long."

"Sure," Holly sighed, resting her chin on her hands.

Cash returned momentarily with a steaming pot of perfectly doughy pillows, slathered in a delicately cozy rose sauce. He handed

Holly a pair of sterling silver pasta tongs which she obligingly accepted.

"What's that look about, Holls? I know you're dying to tell me something."

"I picked up these darling ornaments on Madison Avenue," Holly boasted as her carefully portion controlled ravioli slid onto her plate. "Made from organic, plant-based ivory."

"Plant-based ivory is a thing?"

"It's the only thing, Darling Bear. Every purchase literally saves the life of an African elephant. And it matches the customized tinsel I bought for the tree which is equally important."

"Wow," Cash said after swallowing a slippery ravioli noodle. "That's... specific."

"I thought we'd put the tree in that corner," Holly said, pointing to a spot currently occupied by an ornamental wisteria arrangement in a tall, ceramic jug. "Christmas Eve, we'll be snuggling up with our official tree-trimming sushi."

"I've always meant to ask," Cash said, swirling some wine in a glass. "What does sushi have to do with Christmas?"

"It's tradition."

"What about simple little, spontaneous traditions like peppermint cocoa and snuggles?"

"I don't understand."

"Christmas doesn't have to be so... planned. Organized like an efficient drawer of socks."

"Christmas without details and deadlines?" Holly laughed. "That's fresh."

"I'd be happy to just cozy up with you on the couch with a string of popcorn and a stupid snowman movie."

"I like planning," Holly almost pouted. "It's part of the fun."

Cash pursed his lips as Holly took three more bites, pondering. Before he could change his mind he quickly said, "Do you want to go to Prague?"

Holly dropped her fork. "Prague? Where did that come from?"

"I just thought since neither of us have any family commitments for the holidays..."

"Because neither of us has any family..."

"Maybe this year," Cash said eagerly, "we should have a special backdrop. Something spontaneous."

"What for?" Holly asked. "Christmas in my apartment is crazy romantic. The view. All the twinkle. It's like being in a poem. Trust me, everything is going to be..."

Cash blew on a forkful of ravioli and suddenly fed it to Holly as she closed her eyes and savored the bite.

"...perfect," Holly sighed.

"Is it?" Cash asked nervously. "I mean, do you think it could be even better?"

"I don't think so. You used real crab."

"Sure," Cash said, running his fingers anxiously through his hair, "the ravioli is delicious. But do you ever wonder what comes after?"

Holly's forehead furrowed into a maze of confused creases. "Is this your way of saying you made dessert?"

"No," Cash exhaled. "Don't get me wrong. The *dessert* is unbelievable. I'm just wondering if we should... you know. Make sauce together. Maybe have some little raviolis?"

Holly gawked at Cash in perplexity, completely missing his innuendo. "I'm... not much of a cook."

Cash fidgeted nervously with his left leg suddenly restless.

"What's going on, Cash? Is the oregano not agreeing with you?"

"I wanted to do this in Prague," Cash muttered. "For the ambiance. I wanted everything to be..."

Cash stopped himself as he looked around the room. Holly's apartment was indeed perfect, with soft music playing, candle flames dancing and the city lights outside piercing through the night sky. Everything around them was elegant and classy.

"Screw Prague," Cash said with epiphany. "Everything in this room... in this moment is exactly spot on."

"Cash, what are you..."

"Kitten, um..."

Holly gasped when Cash started rummaging through his pocket for something. He was sweating and his hands were shaking uncontrollably.

"Oh my God," Holly quavered with wide, glistening eyes.

"Give me a minute," Cash stammered. "I brought something with me. I was waiting for exactly the right…"

"Cash…"

"Holly?" Cash said, locking eyes with Holly. "Would you…"

An abrupt knock at the door made them both deflate.

"… see who's at the door?" Cash groaned.

Holly's insides clenched tightly. She could feel her face flush with annoyance and utter disappointment. Who would interrupt such an earth-shatteringly important moment? She grudgingly slapped her linen napkin on the table and thumped over to the door.

"Who in the world…" Holly snarled under her breath.

When Holly opened the door, she found a scruffy, young woman looking imploringly back at her with a face that was literally scuffed with filth. The unwelcome hooligan wore her mousy hair in a messy ponytail held in place with a rubber band. Snow was melting on her ratty boots that looked like they were proportionally three sizes too large for her petite frame. She wore a bulky turtleneck sweater the color of bile that had several gaping rips and was most likely never washed. Her skintight, acid washed jeans had a tear at the knee and were riding up at the crotch. Over her shoulder was a funky duffel bag which dropped with a thud on the floor.

Holly's jaw dropped in tandem with the thudding bag.

"Hey," the young woman offered.

Holly stood agog with her mouth gaping open. If there were any words to describe her emotions, they huddled in the back of her throat and gagged her.

"Can I come in or whatever?" the young woman asked.

"What..." Holly stammered. "...how?"

"Who is it, Holly?" Cash asked.

"Nobody," Holly answered definitively.

"I'm Ivy," the young woman blurted.

Nobody responded.

"Holly's sister," Ivy added.

"But..." Cash said, confused, "Holly doesn't have a sister."

"You don't tell people about me?" Ivy asked with an expression of genuine hurt.

"Ivy..." Holly said warningly.

"Holly?" Cash asked with raised eyebrows.

"Is this a bad time?" Ivy asked.

"Ivy, why are you here?" Holly hissed.

"To... see you."

"Why?"

"It's Christmas," Ivy blinked.

"Holly, are you going to invite her in?" Cash asked.

"It's been seven years," Ivy pleaded. "I just thought..."

"Holly," Cash said, agog. "You haven't seen your sister in seven years?"

"What kind of trouble are you in?" Holly said unsympathetically.

"None," Ivy said, vigorously shaking her head. "I just..."

"I think you should leave," Holly interrupted.

"Holly, please!" Ivy begged. "I have nowhere else to go!"

"Have you eaten?" Cash asked Ivy.

Ivy smiled shyly.

Holly gaped at Cash in disbelief.

CHAPTER FOUR

Holly stared in disbelief as Ivy scarfed down a ginormous pile of ravioli, sucking sauce from her fingers and smacking her lips loudly as she chewed. A hunk of crab clung sickeningly to the corner of Ivy's mouth and refused to let go even when Ivy irreverently wiped her face with her sleeve. Holly looked ill when Ivy licked her plate clean.

Cash pursed his lips in amusement as Ivy ate enough to feed a family of six.

"Is there more?" Ivy asked with her mouth full.

"Lots," Cash said as he dished more food onto Ivy's plate.

"I'm not hungry," Holly muttered when Cash tried to offer her another scoopful.

"Are you like the butler or something?" Ivy asked Cash.

"The butler," Cash giggled. "That's rich."

"Dr. Bartholomew is my partner," Holly said primly, dabbing the sides of her mouth with a linen napkin.

"He's a doctor?" Ivy said, unbuttoning her jeans. "Awesome. Can you look at this thing on my…"

"Ivy!" Holly hissed. "He's a podiatrist!"

"Jeez!" Ivy said, zipping her jeans. "Sorry. I didn't realize he was religious."

"I'm a foot doctor," Cash giggled good-naturedly.

"Makes me sort of wish I had corns," Ivy said flirtatiously.

Holly dropped her fork impatiently.

"So Doc, do you have a first name?"

"Cash."

"You want me to pay you?" Ivy asked, curling her lip.

"Ivy! Oh my God!" Holly gasped, burying her face in her hands.

"My parents were Johnny Cash fans," Cash explained.

Ivy gaped.

"I got off easy," Cash smirked. "They could have called me Sue."

Holly politely chuckled.

Perplexed, Ivy stared blankly at Cash.

"Ivy," Holly said, breaking the awkward silence, "what have you been doing with yourself?"

"In what sense?"

"When was the last time you had a job?" Holly asked.

Cash cleared his throat conspicuously before changing the subject. "Ivy, before you got here, Holly and I were talking about how gloomy Christmas can be without family. How nice that you showed up when you did."

"Yes," Holly said bitterly. "Your timing is impeccable.

"Are you surprised?" Ivy asked, bouncing in her seat. "I wanted it to be a surprise."

"You are literally the last thing I expected to show up on my doorstep."

"I thought we could do all kinds of Christmas crap together," Ivy bubbled. "Like we did when we was little?"

"I've blocked out most of my childhood," Holly admitted.

"We'd go ice skating," Ivy said, turning eagerly to Cash. "Press our noses against toy shop windows. Watch all them drunk Santas staggering around, peeing in the snow. Being six was awesome."

"I have no recollection of being six," Holly said, trying to maintain composure.

Each sip of champagne made Ivy more flirtatious, which Cash found wildly amusing.

Holly shifted with discomfort.

"Is that your real eye color?" Ivy asked, leaning in a little too close to Cash. "I'll bet they glow in the dark like a cat's."

Cash laughed so hard champagne spewed out of his mouth.

Holly lunged to wipe the champagne from the ivory tablecloth.

"Don't worry about it, Holly," Cash laughed. "You can get it dry cleaned."

"We have company, Cash," Holly stage whispered. "I don't want a stain on my Parisian linens."

"No worries," Ivy beamed as she intentionally spilled champagne on the tablecloth, making Holly wince. "I spill stuff all the time. See? Nobody died."

"You really are something, Ivy," Cash laughed, dabbing his eyes.

"Golly, Doc," Ivy said coyly, giving Cash a playful eyebrow triangle and then gesturing towards a painting on the wall. "You're going to make me turn all red like one of them blood clots."

"Those are not blood clots," Holly grunted. "It's French Expressionism."

Ivy cocked her head with a vacant look on her face.

"Gaspard Lefou?" Holly said exasperatedly. "During his Vermillion Period?"

"Do you have any idea what she just said?" Ivy asked Cash.

"Not a clue," Cash laughed, wiping away tears of hilarity.

Holly's hand shook with nerves and rage as she watched Ivy flirt shamelessly with her boyfriend. A dish dropped from Holly's quivering hands and shattered on the floor. Cash winced as Holly bit her fist to prevent herself from swearing.

"Sue!" Ivy blurted out, laughing. "Hey, I just got that!"

Before Cash could process what was happening, he was being dragged by the sleeve away from the table by Holly. "Excuse us," Holly mumbled as she pulled Cash into her bedroom and slammed the door.

"Holls, why didn't you tell me you had a sister?" Cash asked, rubbing his arm from the red finger marks Holly left on his bicep. "This is kind of odd and wonderful, don't you think?"

"Don't leave me alone with her," Holly pleaded with her eyes saturated in terror.

"It's nice that your sister showed up for Christmas," Cash smiled. "It'll give you two a chance to reconnect."

"You don't know what she's like."

"People can change."

"I was hoping we could have an uncomplicated Christmas with just the two of us, Cash. I had the whole thing planned. Until Ivy threw a monkey wrench into the gourmet yule log."

"Ivy's a bit quirky, sure. But..."

"I can't do this."

"Holly, you've never failed at anything you've ever tried. That's why I fell in love with you. And because you are a remarkable and decent person with a huge heart."

Holly sighed.

"Are you going to disagree with me?" Cash asked, pulling Holly close to his chest.

"No," Holly sulked.

Cash lifted Holly's chin upwards and kissed her.

"Cash?" Holly asked, laying her head on him. "Were you going to ask me something tonight?"

"Maybe," Cash winked. "You know we can't stay in this room all night."

"Why not?"

"You have a guest. And I need to get going. I have patients tomorrow."

"You promised you wouldn't leave me here to fend for myself."

"I promised no such thing."

"Cash, you don't know what she's capable of."

"You don't need me here. You're a big girl."

"But Ivy has some kind of wonky personality disorder."

"You are very lucky to have her."

"Why can't you just stay? Please don't go home!"

"You know if I just moved in like we discussed I'd already be home."

"No fair using that as fodder," Holly said, trying to tug Cash back into the bedroom. It was no use. Cash was walking with a purpose back into the dining room and Holly was left with no choice but to follow awkwardly behind him.

"Did you guys have sex in there?" Ivy asked uninhibitedly. "If so, you were disappointingly quiet."

"I have to go," Cash said, putting a brotherly hand on Ivy's shoulder.

"Wait, don't you live here?" Ivy asked. "It seems weird that you're sneaking out for quickies in the middle of dinner, but you're not shacked up."

"We were conversing," Holly explained patiently.

"Is that a fancy word for boinking?" Ivy asked innocently.

Cash hid a smirk behind his hand as Holly assumed a look of utter horror.

"I will see you again, Ivy," Cash said, chivalrously kissing her hand.

"Cash!" Holly shrieked. "Don't put your mouth on that! You don't know where it's been."

"Isn't she funny?" Ivy asked Cash, gazing at Holly dotingly.

"She's a real hoot," Cash teased. "Later, Ladies."

"WaitnoCashnobutCashwaitjustgah," Holly pleaded frantically. She slinked down the closed door into a ball of despair when Cash was gone.

CHAPTER FIVE

Aggressively fluffing a pillow, Holly looked like a stewing thug, sucker-punching someone in the face. Ivy sort of felt sorry for the pillow but she was mesmerized by the plushy, comfy, perfectly arranged bed that Holly prepared for her on the couch. Holly's second-best sheets were neatly tucked into the leathery couch cushions like that of an efficient, Swiss hotel. The quilted blanket was turned down hospitably in geometrical perfection.

"You have lots of nice stuff," Ivy said, looking around.

"Thank you," Holly said, punching the pillow harder. "I work hard. People who work hard get nice stuff. It's sort of a thing."

"Everything matches."

"Is that going to pose a problem?"

"Nope. You like ivory, huh?"

"Nothing wrong with ivory."

"Not at all. Your apartment looks very virginal."

Holly stretched the pillow with indignity.

"Cash seems nice," Ivy observed. "Are you guys porking?"

Shocked, Holly accidentally ripped the pillow open, causing feathers to fly everywhere. Ivy watched with wonder as the feathers floated to the floor.

"I like feathers," Ivy beamed.

"I'll get another pillow."

"Are you okay, Holly?"

"Peachy."

"Really? 'Cause you're kind of making a face."

"Can you do me a favor and not say *porking* in my living room?"

"Sure, Chief. Your place, your rules."

"Nice and comfy," Holly said, plunking a new pillow at the head of the couch.

Ivy's face melted like a disappointed ice-cream cone.

"Is something wrong?" Holly sighed.

"Nah. This is a very nice couch."

"I agree. It's genuine leather."

"I'm pretty sure my back won't give. I've got a slippy disc. I mean as far as couches go..."

"Ivy," Holly said, pinching the top of her nose to stave off an inevitable migraine. "Is this your way of saying you don't want to sleep on the couch?"

"Is that *your* way of offering me the bed?"

Cocking her head in disbelief, Holly squinted at Ivy as she made a beeline for the bedroom and did a cannonball onto Holly's bed.

"Silk sheets?" Ivy bounded. "Er mer gerd!"

Barely resisting the urge to confiscate the sheets from her filthy sister, Holly watched Ivy writhe around like a cartoonish buffoon in the luxurious bedding. "Do... do you want to shower before bed or..."

"Nope!" Ivy bubbled. "I'm good, thanks."

"Really? Because the shower is literally right there in the bathroom."

"Good to know!"

"I'll... I'll be on the couch if you need anything."

"You don't gotta' sleep on the couch," Ivy said, hugging a pillow like a twelve-year- old girl at a slumber party. "Hop in! We can snuggle."

Holly's lips parted, aghast. "Ivy, I... don't really know you."

"Don't you want to talk or whatever? I miss being sisters."

"Honey, other than a coincidence involving DNA, we're strangers."

"But we don't gotta' be. What do you want to do for Christmas? Can we get a tree?"

"It's almost three in the morning. I have to get up early."

"Why?"

"Because I have a job."

"Well, there's that."

Holly exhaled and tried to leave the room.

"Do you got any cheese?" Ivy asked.

"Can it wait until tomorrow?"

"It's sort of an emergency."

"You're having a *cheese emergency?*"

"It's complicated."

Pursing her lips in frustration Holly exhaled, "Wait here."

Ivy craned her neck to make sure Holly was well out of sight before unzipping her duffel bag. A sniffling, little rodent nose peeped out.

"The coast is clear, Poindexter," Ivy whispered as a rat scurried out of the bag. "Hungry?" Ivy asked the rat.

When Holly re-entered with a platter of imported cheese, professionally assorted into an ornate pattern, Ivy scrambled to hide Poindexter under the sheets.

"What's this?" Ivy asked, nosing the cheese.

"Cheese."

"It's not orange."

"It's an assortment of European cheeses."

"Do you have any real cheese? Like the kind that comes in the plastic?"

"Ivy, I am so tired right now, I'm going to assume you didn't say that."

A beseeching squeak came from under the blanket. Once Holly had left the room, Ivy broke off a chunk of Appenzeller cheese and offered it secretly to Poindexter.

***

Flopping around on the couch like a sleepless trout, Holly moaned with exhausted frustration. It was nearly 5:00 a.m. Holly had barely slipped into a shallow sleep, and now she would have to get up for work in a little over an hour. She lay on her back, silently asking the ceiling how she could possibly have let her wayward sister manipulate her into sleeping on the couch. It was a beautiful couch. But it was a couch nonetheless and not conducive to Holly's standards of comfort. She missed her memory foam mattress.

A random squeak made Holly's eyeballs scour the room suspiciously. Was it an intruder? Or was the squeak a figment of Holly's fatigued imagination? Given the disturbing events of the evening, Holly's descent into madness was not outside the realm of possibility.

There it was again.

Squeak.

Holly sat bolt upright on the couch, breathing louder than she intended to. She braced herself. Why was she bracing herself? Did she have intentions of confronting an intruder? And with what would she defend herself? A throw cushion? A nativity shepherd? Stiletto heel? A challenging glare?

Without warning, Poindexter darted across the floor with a chunk of pungent cheese in his mouth. Alarmed, Holly shrieked and stood on the couch, wrapping the blanket around herself.

"Oh my God!" Holly shrieked.

Being careful not to walk across the floor near the rat, Holly walked across the couch, using ottomans, end tables and shelves as stepping-stones to make her way across the room. After grabbing an ornamental wisteria branch, she walked back across the furniture, poising the branch as a weapon.

"Hold still, you disgusting little conduit of disease."

Holly lunged at Poindexter with a blood curdling battle cry. Ivy bolted into the room just in time to witness Holly trying to impale her beloved pet. Ivy screamed like an unrefined banshee, causing Holly to slip off the coffee table, missing the rat completely.

"No!" Ivy wailed in horror, chasing Poindexter and collecting him in her arms for a cuddle.

"Why are you snuggling vermin?" Holly panted.

"His name is Poindexter!"

"Don't name things that carry the Bubonic Plague!"

"He's my friend!"

"This was not part of the arrangement!" Holly railed. "You didn't say anything about rats!"

"You didn't specifically ask if I brought a rat in my duffel bag!"

"This being an Upper East End apartment overlooking Central Park, I felt the no-pestilence rule was implied!"

"If the rat goes, I go!"

Holly made an inadvertent, angry duck face before grabbing Ivy's duffel bag and tossing it out the apartment door. "Out!"

"Maybe I should rephrase..."

"You have overstayed your welcome, Ivy."

"Already? But I practically just got here."

"You weren't invited in the first place."

"Of course not. If you invited me then it wouldn't be a surprise."

"Being ambushed by a saltwater crocodile would also be a surprise. Surprises are not always pleasant. You showing up uninvited would be one of those times."

"You're good at analogies."

"Don't try to charm me. I don't want you here."

"But where will I..."

"Not my problem."

"I promise I..."

"And get that rat out of here," Holly said, dragging Ivy into the hallway, "before he infests my apartment with fleas."

"Don't let it hurt your feelings, Poindexter. She don't know you the way I do."

After slamming the door in Ivy's face, Holly thought twice about leaving her sister alone in the hall. Torn, she reached for the door handle then stopped. Holly guiltily banged her head against the door.

CHAPTER SIX
(SIX DAYS BEFORE CHRISTMAS)

The sleep gods were indeed sadistic. Holly had only been asleep for twenty minutes when her alarm clock woke her with a heart-stopping buzzer. Holly found herself tangled in the dirty mess of sheets that Ivy left behind on her bed. Exhausted, Holly emerged from her blankets, finding chunks of cheese and fur in awkward places in the sheets and pillow. The daylight that streaked through the window blinds exposed more clearly how filthy the bedding was after Ivy's brief encounter.

Grimacing and grunting, Holly showered, dressed in her professional attire and drowsily lumbered into the kitchen to fill her travel mug with coffee. In mid-stride, Holly caught a glimpse of the floppy, red hat Ivy left behind.

"Oh Ivy," Holly sighed guiltily.

Did she do the right thing casting her little sister out in the cold in the wee hours of the morning? Travel mug in hand, Holly opened the apartment door to leave for work. She was startled when she found Ivy, sound asleep in the hall with Poindexter snoozing on her shoulder.

"God!" Holly gasped.

Ivy awoke with a start.

"Ivy, did you sleep here all night?"

"Don't feel bad," Ivy yawned. "That was the most comfortable sleep I've had in a long while. The night before last I slept in a dumpster in Greenwich Village."

"Get off the floor. This is unseemly."

"I like your pant suit."

"Thank you. Now get in the apartment before someone sees you."

"For reals? I can stay?"

"Obviously I can't set my little sister loose in New York with nowhere to go. Not with decision making skills like yours."

"What about Poindexter? The rat and I are a two-fer."

"Whatever," Holly said, massaging her temples.

"Gee, that's swell. Poindexter's never been to New York before. Plus this is his first Christmas." Ivy nuzzled Poindexter. "Say thank you to Auntie Holly."

"Really?" Holly said, rolling her eyes.

"Why don't you play hooky?" Ivy bubbled. "We'll call up Cash and the four of us'll go wassailing."

"I have to go to work, Hun."

"All day?"

"I'm a grown up, Ivy. I have to..." Holly sighed and gave Ivy some money from her purse. "Poindexter's never been to New York? Show him a good time. Take in a show or something. I'll be home around eight. Hopefully."

"By myself? I don't know my way around Manhattan. What if I get mugged?"

Mentally critiquing Ivy's clothes and musing on how she had the fashion sense of a vagrant, Holly tried not to comment. She couldn't help it though.

"You have nothing to worry about."

Ivy's brow furrowed with worry.

"Here," Holly sighed, handing Ivy her cell phone. "Christmas time in Manhattan is like a fairy tale for grownups. Pretty lights. Shopping. Random celebrity sightings. Central Park is right outside. You could wonder around there all day like a free range chicken."

Holly was caught off guard when Ivy suddenly hugged her.

"Thanks for everything, Sis," Ivy said tearfully. "I love you somethin' fierce."

"Sure," Holly said, softening. "Have a good day. Call me with this phone if you need anything. I'll find something for us to do after work."

"Promise?"

"Please," Holly said as she headed down the hall, "have a shower."

Ivy beamed.

***

Cash could hear the shower running when he let himself into Holly's apartment.

"Holls?" he called into the empty room. He placed a dozen red roses on the kitchen counter, then paused when he heard the shower stop running. Cash needed to decide quickly. He took a ring box out of his pocket, turning it around in his fingers for a moment. Taking a deep breath, Cash headed towards the bathroom door.

"Kitten?" Cash called, rapping on the bathroom door with his knuckle. "I want to show you something."

Freshly showered Ivy suddenly popped out of the bathroom, wearing a skimpy towel around her middle, leaving very little up to the imagination. Cash gasped and scrambled to put the ring back in his pocket. He squeezed his eyes shut and tried to look in any direction other than where Ivy was standing. Ivy, on the other hand, stood shamelessly dripping without so much as an embarrassed blush.

"Ivy!" Cash squeaked. "I am so sorry!"

"Hey Doc," Ivy said casually, still dripping. Still farcically exposed. "What did you want to show me?"

"You're... clean."

"Squeaky."

"I... I thought you were Holly," Cash said awkwardly, still having no idea where to look. "I should go."

"Why?" Ivy said grabbing Cash's arm and not caring that doing so let her towel slip farther down her front. "We could hang out. Holly gave me money. And one of her phones. She's going to be at work all day so..."

"I have patients."

"Okay. Then we can wait for her."

"No," Cash stammered, trying so hard not to look directly at Ivy. "I mean I have to be at my office. I have people depending on me."

"What is it with you two and work?"

"I... This isn't right. I should just be elsewhere."

"Is this because of my knockers?"

"I should go."

"You don't gotta' be embarrassed. I'm not."

"Ivy..."

"It's just body parts. Like elbows."

"Um..." Cash quavered in a failed attempt to not laugh.

"Look, if you're one of them prudish dudes I'll put on some pants. Will that help?"

Cash's cheek dimpled.

"You look good in red, Doc," Ivy winked as she pulled on some acid washed jeans.

Cash suddenly realized how flushed his face felt.

After pulling on her itchy, green sweater Ivy sniffed the air, discovering an intriguing aroma wafting over from Cash. Ivy sniffed Cash, who was a little unsure about how he should feel about being sniffed.

"What smells?" Ivy asked, scrunching her nose.

"Are you sniffing me?"

"You smell like frankincense."

"Good nose."

"It's kind of arousing."

"Frankincense is one of Holly's Christmas fragrances."

Cash was in physical pain trying to suppress laughter as Ivy's head dreamily nestled into Cash's chest.

"Mmm," Ivy moaned. "I wish I had me a man who smelled like you."

Amused, Cash peeled Ivy off his body.

"If you like this," Cash smirked, "next time I'll wear the myrrh."

"Myrrh!" Ivy howled as though it was the most charmingly hilarious thing she had ever heard.

Cash shook his head amicably and smiled, sizing Ivy up and down. Before he headed out, he gave Ivy another one of his signature smooches on the hand. Ivy tingled.

"It's nice to have you around, Ivy."

"Sure," Ivy said giddily.

Ivy watched Cash dreamily as he walked out the door. His pants. Wow.

CHAPTER SEVEN

A floppy Santa's hat adorned Philomena's head as she spotted Holly approaching, pristine as usual but with a caffeinated shark stare and shadows of exhaustion lurking beneath her bloodshot eyes.

"What in the world..." Philomena trailed.

"Rough night," Holly said bluntly.

"Oh dear. Deadline insomnia?"

"I'd prefer not to talk about it."

Philomena wriggled eagerly as though awaiting a slab of juicy gossip.

"Did you order flight tickets for Anuj?" Holly asked, trying to ignore Philomena's animated curiosity. "I need him to represent me at the conference in Yazoo City on the twenty-first. I'll be tied up here..."

"You always tell me everything," Philomena said sideways. "If you'd prefer not to talk about it, you must be hiding something delicious."

Holly stood, exasperated for a moment, lolling her eyeballs in the direction of an invisible deity who might be willing to spare a shred of mercy. "My sister showed up. Like poof! Out from nowhere."

"You don't have a sister," Philomena pointed out.

"That's what I kept telling myself."

"What do you mean your *sister* showed up."

"At my door. In the middle of what might have been my engagement had she not..."

"Whoa..."

"I know."

"You mean Cash..."

"... was gearing up to put a big shiny one on my finger."

"But then..."

"Ivy..."

"Who's Ivy?"

"My estranged sister."

Philomena formed an exaggerated letter O with her mouth.

"Ivy thinks she's staying for Christmas."

"What are you going to do?"

"What *can* I do? I let her stay. Cash made me."

"What... you know... happened between the two of you?"

"I don't want to go into that. Not here."

"Is there… something wrong with her?"

"Likely."

"So she's…"

"Trouble. Deranged. Toxic."

"Wow."

"So much wow."

"Where is she now?"

"At my place. Hopefully showering. Ugh."

"Are you sure that's safe? To be leaving her alone?"

"It's never safe to leave her alone. She's a ninnyhammer."

"Can she go anywhere else?"

"She says she has nowhere else to go. I honestly have no idea what else to do. She'll likely sleep on the street otherwise. Not my problem, I know. But she… well."

"But what are you going to do with a… with a…"

"Ruffian."

"…with a ruffian for Christmas?"

"Survive, hopefully. Other than that, I have absolutely no idea. Ivy is a stranger. She does not fit into my carefully planned holiday."

"Speaking of which," Philomena said, clacking her festive fingernails on her computer keyboard, "I have a notice to remind you about the Podiatry Holiday Banquet this coming Saturday."

"Whuuut," Holly groaned.

"You committed to it three months ago," Philomena shrugged. "You told me to put it on my calendar in case you forgot. You forgot, didn't you?"

"That was before Brower and Port sprung the whole eggnog thing on us."

"But Cash already bought the tickets. Four hundred dollars a pop."

"Seriously? Why would tickets to a Christmas staff party..."

"The proceeds go towards sending orthopedic shoes to orphans in Lesotho."

"Wow. That's altruistic."

"You're not going to stand Cash up..."

"You don't seriously think I can manage..."

"Holly..."

"Look, I didn't plan for this. When I committed to this banquet, I calculated that my presentation yesterday would be followed by a few days of relative downtime before Christmas. I didn't mean for this..."

"Holly, it's Christmas. And Cash is so proud of you. Don't make him go by himself without an elegant lady to show off to his peers."

"Can you tell him for me?"

Philomena's lips parted.

"Thanks, Mena."

Holly trotted into her office before the shock had a chance to melt off Philomena's face.

***

Poindexter peeped out of Ivy's pocket as Ivy, wide-eyed, explored New York City. The crisp air numbed her face as she stumbled gracelessly among the throng of bustling New Yorkers. She had just left a hipster espresso bar where she was ripped off by being offered a ridiculously small cup of coffee for quadruple the price she expected. She was also stunned by the tarry flavor and texture of the coffee which she irreverently spewed from her mouth. She was asked to leave which she willingly did, promising a lawsuit for nearly poisoning her.

Once she finally got the rancid espresso flavor out of her mouth, she approached a mad prophet on the street, wearing a sandwich sign. He was condemning everyone to the inevitable demise of Hell where there will be wailing and gnashing of teeth. Ivy turned pale and dropped her jaw in horror, then ran flailing down the street screaming, *"We're all going to die!"*

While losing her mind with terror, she turned a sharp corner on to Madison Avenue. Having the attention span of a goldfish, Ivy was distracted by the window of a high-end store. Perhaps delaying her inevitable demise foretold by the oracle on the corner, Ivy slipped into the store and ogled the incredibly expensive clothes. She ran her fingers over the fabrics as though the garments were spun from pure gold. In her wildest dreams she could never afford even one sleeve. Quick as a ninja, Ivy swiped a few sweaters and stuffed them in her duffel bag.

***

Barging abruptly into Holly's office Rex intrusively handed Holly a perfume sample. "Sniff," he ordered.

Holly took a whiff of the perfume sample. "Gross," she said, her nose wrinkling from an offensive odor that stung her nostrils.

"Sulphuric, right?" Rex nodded angrily. "This is what happens when you try to simulate the scent of eggnog."

"That's supposed to be eggnog?" Holly grimaced. "It smells more like an expired egg salad sandwich."

"Me and the guys were up all night, Holly."

"Me too," Holly yawned.

"This isn't going to happen."

"You know what, leave the prototype with me. I'm taking some other samples home with me to analyze."

Holly's cell phone rang. She tried to ignore it.

"Rex, I'm meeting with Brower and Port tomorrow…"

The phone rang again.

"It's my sister," Holly groaned.

"Call her back when the world isn't ending."

"I suspect she's in some kind of trouble."

"This is not over, Holly," Rex barked with an accusing finger in her face. "Don't you dare pick up that call… She's picking up the call."

"Ivy?" Holly said on the phone.

"Holly, I'm lost in New York City," Ivy sobbed on the phone from a bustling city street.

"Calm down, Ivy," Holly said dully, rubbing her eyelids. "Tell me where you are and I'll talk you home."

"If I knew where I was I wouldn't be lost. Help, Holly. It's weird here. I just saw a guy burst into song for absolutely no reason."

"It's Manhattan," Holly said, silently shooing Rex away. "People do that. Ivy, listen to me. Look around. Be aware of your surroundings. Can you see a street sign? A conspicuous landmark?"

"Um…" Ivy said, looking around nervously. "There's people everywhere? There's ice skating? Horses and buggies? And I think I saw penguins and Robert Burns and a Chinese guy playing a zither."

"Ivy," Holly exhaled putting in an extreme effort to be patient, "you're not lost. You're in Central Park. Look to the left. You can see my apartment building from where you are standing."

"I don't see it," Ivy said, looking around. "This park is frickin' huge and smells like sausages. I've been walking around here for hours. Like three or four of them."

Another call beeped on Holly's phone.

"Keep wandering around," Holly enunciated much too clearly. "You'll eventually find your way back."

Holly checked the call display for the incoming call.

Brower and Port.

"I'm confused, Holly," Ivy whimpered. "Please come and get me."

"Leave work in the middle of the day?" Holly said sarcastically. "I'm not your babysitter."

"Nobody said you were my babysitter," Ivy pouted, insulted.

"You know what?" Holly said impatiently. "Go to the Guggenheim."

"What's a Guggenheim?" Ivy asked.

Holly hung up.

* * *

Foot fungus was not Cash's favorite. Which was why he was slightly relieved – albeit slightly embarrassed – to hear Holly's distinct ring tone on his cell. *"I Just Called to Say I Love You"* by Stevie Wonder.

"I um…" Cash said with the patient's foot still in his hands. "I should get that."

"Clearly," the patient smirked.

"Hey Kitten," Cash purred, making the patient pretend to gag himself. "Can I call you back? I'm treating a fungal..." Cash's jaw dropped when he realized who was sobbing on the phone. "...Ivy?"

"What's a Guggenheim?" Ivy quipped in a panic on the phone, looking dizzily around Central Park as though she was inside a salad spinner.

"What's going on?" Cash asked, using his hand to screen himself from the eavesdropping patient.

"I'm in trouble. I didn't know who else to call?"

"Where are you? I'll be right there."

Cash shrugged apologetically at his squinting patient.

CHAPTER EIGHT

"Sorry for the trouble," Ivy said, huddled next to Cash in the back seat of a taxi. "Manhattan's a bit of an ADHD nightmare."

"It's no trouble, Ivy," Cash reassured her. "You're family."

"Gee," Ivy blushed.

"So where would you like to go?" Cash asked, rubbing his hands together eagerly. "South Street Seaport? Maybe a Yankee's game?"

"I thought you had patients."

"I cleared my schedule for the day."

"You can do that?"

"How often do I have family in town?" Cash smiled jovially. "It's Christmas for God's sake."

"Don't you have family?" Ivy asked.

"I lost my mom and dad several years ago."

"Jeez," Ivy said empathetically. "Do you want me to help you look for them?"

After a perplexed beat, Cash burst into an explosion of laughter.

Ivy gaped, having no idea what was funny.

"It's awful nice of you to stop everything for the likes of me," Ivy said bashfully. "I got a feeling Holly would never do that. Not for me, anyway."

"You caught her off guard, Ivy. She wasn't expecting to have her sister in town."

"But still."

"Don't take it personally, okay? She isn't meaning to blow you off."

"I don't think Holly likes me."

"I'm sure she…" Cash hesitated. "I'm sure underneath…"

"I'm not all that likable."

"That's not true, Ivy."

"Sure it is. I reek of trouble. And sweaty pits."

Cash sprayed laughter across the taxi. "Look, I don't know what happened between you and Holly. And maybe it's none of my business… Well, I wish Holly had said something about you but…"

"She's ashamed of me. She don't want me here for Christmas. I guess I made another one of my world famous indiscretions. Is that a word?"

"It's not that she doesn't want…" Cash hesitated again. "See, Holly has this system…"

"Why doesn't Holly have no Christmas tree?" Ivy asked in one of her distracted episodes.

"That's all part of Holly's strategy," Cash explained. "The tree goes up on Christmas Eve at 7:30 pm. 8:00 is the inspection to ensure that the decorations have been hung symmetrically. Then she orders the official tree trimming sushi. Kappa maki, pufferfish and freshwater eel."

"That don't sound so festive," Ivy said, scrunching her nose. "Why do you go along with it?"

"Because, Ivy. Holly's worth it. She's my girl."

Ivy lowered her head. "Holly's rules are dumb. What's the point of having a tree if you just have to take it down right after?"

"Right?" Cash chimed. "I keep telling her that."

"The tree's like the whole point of Christmas. It gets you all excited. In the mood. Christmas is over in no time flat. Waiting for Christmas is the fun part. Without a Christmas tree what's the freaking point of Christmas at all?"

"This Christmas tree really means a lot to you, doesn't it?"

"Kind of," Ivy admitted. "Reminds me a bit of when Holly and I used to be sisters."

Cash felt his heart sink. An idea suddenly glimmered in his eye, followed by a conspiratorial dimple. "Rockefeller Center," Cash instructed the driver.

The taxi picked up speed as Ivy looked out the side window with childlike wonder. "Where are we going, Doc?"

"I'll never tell," Cash winked. "I've got a big surprise for you."

"Are you going to sell me as a slave to the Ishmaelites like that guy in the Bible?" Ivy asked, edging slowly away from Cash.

"Ivy!" Cash howled with laughter. "Of course not!"

"Then what are you up to? I'm not sure about this."

"Hasn't anyone ever done something nice for...you?" Cash turned pale when he realized that the answer was probably no. "Ivy," Cash said, rubbing her back comfortingly, "You are going to love this. I promise."

Ivy's eyes widened like saucers when she saw something out the window. Gasping with desperate excitement, she threw open the taxi door and hurled herself out of the vehicle before it came to a complete stop.

"Ivy!" Cash screamed, begging the driver to stop and then running from the taxi to catch up with Ivy who was ogling the ginormous Christmas tree outside the Rockefeller Center. The glowing ornaments reflected on her eyeballs as she stared in awe like a little girl with sparkles of magic in her smile.

"Are you seeing this right now?" Ivy shrieked.

"Yes," Cash laughed breathlessly, catching up. "Do you like it?"

"*Do I?* This big-arse pine could house an extended family of Catholic squirrels!"

Cash caught himself staring at Ivy whose eyes were glowing with wonder. She was shivering. Cash impulsively took a pair of irresistibly fluffy earmuffs, not unlike Holly's furry hat, out of a shopping bag he was carrying and put them on Ivy's ears.

"Here," Cash smiled.

"What are these?" Ivy asked, feeling the furry wonderfulness.

"Designer earmuffs. Merry Christmas."

"You bought these for me?"

"I bought them for Holly. But you looked so cold so…"

"It is kinda' nippy out here. Are you sure though? Holly's your main squeeze."

"Holly has way more than she needs. Besides, I can get her something else. She doesn't have to know," Cash winked.

Ivy felt the earmuffs in amazement, feeling the kittenishly soft faux fur slide over her fingertips. She had never felt anything so luxurious. She turned eagerly to face Cash who was glistening from the lights on the tree. He looked irresistible.

"Say Doc…"

"Don't call me that unless you have a foot malady. I'm Cash."

"Cool," Ivy said, realizing that her voice sounded drifty. She collected herself, realizing her voice probably shouldn't sound drifty. "I was just wondering. Did Holly mention to you why we haven't seen each other in seven years?"

"No."

"Maybe…" Ivy said, swallowing hard. "…maybe I should…"

"I don't want to know," Cash said bluntly.

"You don't?"

"It doesn't matter now, Ivy. You and Holly are lucky to have each other. You're together. That's all that matters."

Ivy smiled shyly although she was still shivering. Cash put a brotherly arm around her to keep her warm.

"Yeah," Ivy said, unsure.

CHAPTER NINE

"Shih tzu!"

As Philomena was preparing to leave for the evening, she stiffened when she heard Holly causing a loud commotion from inside her office.

"Holly?" Philomena called from her desk. "Why are you hollering expletives in there?"

Scurrying out of her office with her coat half on, Holly scrambled frantically past Philomena's desk that was glowing like a festive dollar store window display. "I told my sister I'd be home by eight! Damn! She's probably set herself on fire by now!"

"I'm sure she's fine," Philomena reassured her. "She never called back."

Holly stopped in her tracks, paled by panic. "Even more reason to worry. What if she broke, lost or pawned my cell phone? She could be soiling my upholstery. Or smoking the alfalfa sprouts in my crisper."

"Mr. Brower stopped by my desk about an hour ago," Philomena said, trying to snap Holly out of her anxiety-induced trancelike state. "He wanted me to tell you that he bumped the meeting up by one hour tomorrow morning."

"Of course he did," Holly grunted, trying to brisk walk towards the elevator."

"Don't forget the perfume samples!" Philomena called after her.

*　*　*

The sky was quickly darkening, and the snow was blowing around in a funnel of ornery wind as Holly ran ridiculously down the street in her tragically impractical boots.

"Taxi!" she screamed, her voice squeaking and strangled against the gusts. Every single taxi whooshed by without stopping. When she slipped unceremoniously on a sidewalk crack, a perfume sample fell out of Holly's bag and rolled down the street.

"NO!"

Holly spotted the perfume bottle in a mound of slush in the road. She winced every time a car narrowly missed the bottle. She frantically lunged towards the street but was prevented from moving forward when a yellow cab pulled up too close to the intersection.

"Sure," Holly groaned sarcastically. "*Now* you stop." Holly pounded ferociously on the hood of the taxi like a rogue grizzly. "Move it!"

Once the taxi had the good sense to screech out of the way, Holly lunged into the street, causing every car on the road to honk and every voice on the street to shout harshly. Tires shrieked. Drivers scolded.

"Stop!" Holly shouted at onlookers. "Watch it! Sorry! What the...!"

Holly skid through the slush and managed to grab the perfume bottle, exhaling with relief, then inhaling and gagging on exhaust fumes.

***

"Ivy?" Holly called feebly, unscrewing her mangled feet from her sadistic boots. She was disheveled. "I'm home, Hun."

No answer.

Holly looked around the room, finding the television on. She could hear Ivy laughing but her wayward sister was nowhere to be found.

"I have a fun evening planned," Holly continued. "I thought we'd make organic bison chili. Sorry I'm..."

Holly turned to find Ivy and Cash on the couch together, laughing and stringing popcorn with a movie on in the background. Holly's eyes widened with surprise at how chummy her sister was with her boyfriend. Or more accurately, how chummy Cash was with Ivy.

"...late..." Holly trailed off.

"Holly!" Ivy said happily, bouncing her butt on the couch. "I got earmuffs!"

Holly's lips parted. Ivy was indeed wearing earmuffs. And said earmuffs were at the top of the Christmas list she had emailed to Cash.

"They look good on her, don't they Kitten?" Cash said with the widest grin Holly had ever seen. Or at least it seemed that way to Holly.

"What are you..." Holly quavered.

"We're stringing popcorn and watching a stupid snowman movie," Ivy laughed, lolling her eyeballs flirtatiously at Cash.

Holly looked stung.

"Cash rescued me," Ivy actually sounded proud of herself.

"Excuse me, he did what now?"

"She got my number from your phone," Cash explained.

"She just called you up and you just... you just left work? That's preposterous, Cash. You had patients today."

"I moved some appointments around. It was no big deal."

"He showed me around New York. We went to Time Square and I hugged a Smurf."

"And now you're... you're doing this? On the couch?"

"Holly, why are you being weird?" Cash said, shifting.

"Popcorn strings?" Holly said accusingly. "A stupid snowman movie? Cash, I thought we..."

"You didn't want to," Cash shrugged.

Holly took a deep breath and opened the fridge to put her perfume samples inside. "It's... it's nice to see you two are getting along. Especially, Cash, since you certainly didn't have to..."

"It was my pleasure," Cash said, patting Ivy's little hand. "Ivy is a lot of fun. And I doubt I would have had a chance to see the Rockefeller tree at all this year had Ivy not called me up."

Holly held her breath in for longer than what is probably considered responsible. "Happy for you. Cash will you be joining us for…"

Holly gaped when she realized that other than her perfume samples, the fridge had nothing inside.

"The fridge is completely empty," Holly blankly stated the obvious.

"I snarfed some breakfast this morning," Ivy admitted unapologetically. "Want some popcorn?"

Holly gawked at Ivy in disbelief as she watched Ivy shove fistfuls of popcorn into her mouth — and into Cash's mouth — and Poindexter's mouth.

"You ate the entire contents of my fridge?" Holly asked through clenched teeth. "Enough food to feed three people for the next seven days? *For breakfast?*"

"Holly, it's not a big deal," Cash said.

"What are we going to eat, Cash? The rat?"

"Hey!" Ivy protested.

"We'll be spontaneous," Cash shrugged. "We'll order calzones."

"It's bison chili night," Holly protested. I had all the ingredients ready in the fridge. My mouth was watering for it all day."

"Well, it's not happening tonight," Cash sighed. "We'll eat something equally fun."

"Nothing is equally fun as bison chili."

"Calzones are fun."

"Bison is a lean alternative..."

"So we'll get bison calzones."

"That's not a thing. Stop making things up."

"You can put anything in a calzone."

"Untrue."

"You literally can."

"What about pantyhose? Can you put pantyhose in a calzone?"

"If someone had a taste for that kind of thing, I'm sure Angelo's would accommodate."

"You've taken leave of your senses."

"You're the one who preplans meals three weeks in advance."

Ivy's head turned back and forth between Holly and Cash as they bantered like a perturbed tennis ball.

"Cash, why do you have to make light of..."

"Because it's *no big deal.*"

"Perhaps you failed to notice that I have an indefinite houseguest and wait for it... *no food in the fridge.*"

"So go shopping."

"Don't be ignorant."

"How is that ignorant?"

"I can't go shopping, Cash."

"Why?"

"Because it's not Wednesday."

"She only shops on Wednesdays?" Ivy interjected.

"Holly has her way of doing things."

"I have many important tasks to juggle," Holly defended herself. "Shopping on a different day would throw off my biorhythms."

"Then I'll shop for you," Cash offered. "Make a list for me. I'll go tomorrow."

"Ivy," Holly sighed. "At any point in time was there a little voice in your head, suggesting that other people in this home might also like something to eat?"

"No voices," Ivy shook her head. "Sorry."

"Ivy..." Holly quaked.

"Who wants Chinese?" Cash abruptly changed the subject, much to the chagrin of Holly.

Ivy quickly put up her hand with a girlish gasp.

"I was going to make us a wholesome meal," Holly muttered.

"Nothing's more fun than eating out of little boxes," Cash beamed. "With sticks."

"Am I the only one," Holly heaved, "who sees how completely selfish…"

"Holly…" Cash warned.

"Ivy, I have tried to be a gracious host…"

"Holls, come on. Ivy hasn't had a proper meal in weeks."

"Can we get chicken balls?" Ivy asked dreamily.

"Yes," Cash answered quickly.

"Thanks, Casherson," Ivy gushed.

"Casherson?" Holly said, curling her lip in revulsion.

"Holly…" Cash warned.

"Why is she calling my boyfriend Casherson?"

"It's cute," Cash said, trying to be discreet. "Why are you being like this?"

"Why are the two of you flirting your faces off on my couch?" Holly's voice cracked.

"We're not flirting," Cash said evenly.

"She's throwing herself at you!"

"Should I leave or whatever?" Ivy deflated.

Cash said no at the same moment that Holly said yes. Cash and Holly looked at each other. Cash shook his head disappointedly at Holly.

"I didn't mean to…" Ivy stammered.

"I never pegged you as someone who would fling your own sister out in the cold like a sack of dead pigeons," Cash said, pointing his index finger deep into Holly's chest.

Overwhelmed, Holly struggled for words, then she caught a glimpse of a messily giftwrapped present underneath a fern.

"What's that?" Holly said, nearly inaudibly.

"I got you a Christmas present," Ivy said sheepishly.

"You did?" Holly asked humbly.

"You don't got a tree," Ivy said apologetically. "So I put it under a fern."

Holly's mouth gaped stupidly for a moment. "I... I didn't know we were exchanging."

"Sure we are! Or at least I thought..."

Cash watched Holly intensely as she bit her fist. Perhaps there was a real sister hiding under all those designer clothes. He startled Holly by putting his hand on the small of her back. He was just about to lean down for a smooch when he was rudely interrupted by his cell phone.

CHAPTER TEN

Despite her greatest efforts, Holly could not hide her revulsion as she watched Ivy feeding Poindexter some chop suey from the end of a chopstick.

"Sorry," Ivy apologized after noticing how Holly was trying to force back a sick look. She then offered Holly the same chop suey she had been feeding to her rat. "Did you want some chop suey?"

Holly rapidly shook her head.

"Shame Cash got called in for an emergency hammertoe procedure," Ivy said with her mouth full of bean sprouts. "Stupid people and their hammertoes. Must make you jealous, huh? Cash fondling all them feet?"

"Cash and I are in a committed relationship," Holly said primly, demurely popping a singular shrimp into her mouth.

"What if he was treating one of them shoe models?" Ivy said, leaning in closer to Holly with mischievously dancing eyes.

"It wouldn't matter," Holly said, shifting uncomfortably on the couch.

"Wouldn't it?" Ivy pondered. "I think it would drive me out of my head."

"Can we not talk about feet while we're eating?" Holly asked, discovering something gross on the end of her chopstick. "While we're eating... whatever this is?"

Holly's cell phone buzzed with a text from Cash. *"I'll make it up to you. Tomorrow night. Rooftop. Just you and me."*

Holly smirked coyly.

"Do we have to wait until Christmas Eve?" Ivy suddenly asked.

"For what?"

"A Christmas tree, Doofus. I really, really want one. Like before Christmas is already over."

"What's this obsession you have with Christmas trees?"

"What is this obsession you have with *everything?*"

"Excuse me?"

"Why can't you wear sneakers and sweats once in a while? Throw your hair into a ponytail? Call in sick for no reason? Forget to floss? Shop on a Thursday?"

"Are you implying that I'm uptight?"

"You used the word *biorhythms* in a sentence. And your apartment is like a museum. I'm afraid to sit anywhere."

"I am extremely fun," Holly said in a deathly serious tone.

"Prove it. Let's get a tree. Right now."

"Fine." Holly twitched. She defiantly grabbed her artificial tree from the storage closet and stuck it resentfully in a stand. "Happy?"

"What's that?" Ivy said, cocking her head.

"My Christmas tree."

"It's fake."

"It's a perfectly efficient tree."

"It's not even green."

"You're point being..."

"Trees aren't ivory."

"This one is."

"Why is this tree ivory? That's twisted."

"It matches."

"Your apartment?"

"Of course."

"But why does literally everything in here have to be ivory?"

"Elegance."

"I feel like I'm drowning in a vat of melting, vanilla ice-cream."

"That's offensive."

"But everything's ivory. I'm afraid to spill something on something. What if I spill?"

"The goal is not to spill."

"I don't know if I can live with that kind of stress."

"My place. My color scheme."

"This is really stressful."

"Shut up and enjoy the tree."

"But it's ivory."

"As is the star. And the holly berries. And the tinsel. And the lights. And the sparkly partridges."

"Why though?"

"This is not open for debate. This is my tree and I like it."

"Again, not green."

"Ivy!"

"And it doesn't smell like a tree."

"That's what scented candles are for."

"Migraines."

"What?"

"Let's chop one down?"

"In Manhattan?"

"The folks next door got a real tree. I seen them drag it in yesterday."

"They must have driven to Jersey."

Ivy raised a finger to ask a question.

"No," Holly answered preemptively.

"Fine," Ivy pouted. "Give me some stupid tinsel."

"My tinsel is not stupid. I got it from Bergdorf and Goodman."

"Tinsel? What is it made of? The hair of baby Jesus?"

Ivy grabbed a handful of tinsel and tossed it carelessly on the tree.

"Ivy!" Holly gasped, horrified, grabbing the tinsel from Ivy and applying it to the tree herself. "Hanging tinsel is a delicate art form. Each strand must be gracefully hung. Angled so as to capture the light. Wispy. Ephemeral. Like dainty icicles dripping in the twilight."

Ivy blew the bangs off her forehead as she attempted to hang an ornament, resulting in a grimace from Holly.

"What's wrong?" Ivy sighed. "Doesn't it go there?"

"I usually put that one... you know what, Hun? Why don't I just show you how I like it?"

Ivy plunked herself woefully on the couch, squinting at Holly as she decorated the tree with precision and delicacy. Did she really have to hang the tinsel one strand at a time? Reconfigure the lights two hundred times in order to maximize the twinkle? Polish every single ornament with a special microfiber cloth? Use a protractor to ensure the star topper was geometrically satisfying?

Absolutely bored out of her mind, Ivy slouched on the couch, nibbling a hangnail on her thumb.

"Astonishingly perfect," Holly finally said, stepping back to admire her masterpiece.

"Yup," Ivy said glumly.

"What's your problem?"

"No problem."

"You wanted a tree. I gave you a tree."

"It's a real nice tree."

"Then why are you crumpled on my couch like a miserable basset hound, gnawing on your hand?"

"No reason," Ivy said lifelessly, spitting out a sliver of thumbnail.

"I put the tree up. Isn't that what you wanted?"

"I wanted to decorate the tree together," Ivy moaned toddlerishly.

"Oh come on, don't be like that. I just thought it would be easier..."

"It completely defeats the purpose when you..."

"We would have just bickered."

"... you hogged the whole tree. I didn't even get a turn."

"A turn? What are you, four?"

"I was looking forward to..."

"Why do you always make me out to be a bad person when I'm only trying to..."

"I'm bored."

"Of course you are," Holly said, throwing her hands up.

"You ruined everything."

"I... Ivy, it's just a tree."

"That's the whole point," Ivy said with her voice cracking. "It's *just a tree.* You're not dressing yourself for your wedding. You're not performing brain surgery. You're putting candy canes and glittery partridges on a fake conifer. It's supposed to be fun."

"I like things a certain way."

"Maybe I don't got a fancy education like you," Ivy said, welling with emotion. "And maybe I don't rake in as many digits as you. But it's not fair, you thinking I'm going to mess things up before I even try."

"Ivy..."

"I'm a person, you know. With feelings."

Holly deflated, biting her lower lip in contemplation.

"To think," Ivy sniffed, "I was excited about spending Christmas with my posh sister in New York. I'm just wrecking things."

"Ivy..."

"Don't you have an early meeting tomorrow?" Ivy asked, wiping snot indelicately with her sleeve.

The awkward silence was ringing in Holly's ears like guilty sirens. Her lungs constricted as she took a deep breath. "It's been a long time since I've been a sister," Holly admitted. "I don't really know what I'm doing."

"Neither do I," Ivy squeaked. "But at least I'm trying.

CHAPTER ELEVEN
(FIVE DAYS BEFORE CHRISTMAS)

Holly brisk-walked past Philomena's desk.

"Mena, can you run out on your lunch break and pick up a Christmas gift for my sister?" Holly asked. "Apparently we're exchanging."

"What does she want?" Philomena asked, revealing an ugly Christmas sweater with a protruding reindeer on the front.

"I don't know," Holly admitted.

"She's your sister," Philomena pointed out. "If you don't know what she wants, how am I supposed to know?"

Holly looked at her watch and winced.

"Use one of my credit cards," Holly instructed. And in terms of price... Ouch. I should have been in the boardroom eleven minutes ago."

Holly hurried into the boardroom, pulling off her furry hat to reveal some volatile hairs drifting statically from her head. She hastily flattened them.

"Thank you for your patience," Holly said, maintaining composure. "I take full accountability for the eleven wasted minutes. But I assure you, what I have prepared will make the inconvenience seem insignificant."

Brower and Port looked at each other, grunting with annoyance.

"The lab has been working tirelessly on the new fragrance," Holly continued.

"Do you have the prototype?" Brower snorted while steepling his fingers.

"I'm five steps ahead of you, Mr. Brower. I analyzed the scents last night and..."

Holly opened her bag and turned pale.

"Is something wrong?" Port groaned.

"It seems I left the samples at home."

Brower and Port furrowed their brows and fidgeted impatiently.

"I know this looks bad," Holly involuntarily stammered. "Really. Bad. But when you hear what happened you'll have a good chortle. You see, my wayward sister..."

Philomena discreetly popped her head into Holly's office.

"Holly?" Philomena stage whispered. "You sister just called me."

"This is the worst possible time," Holly hissed.

"Holly..." Philomena tried again.

"Mr. Brower? Port? Excuse me for a moment, will you?... Mena, how could Ivy possibly know..."

"You left your cell on my desk," Philomena apologized. "I think you should..."

"Tell her I can't..."

"She's dying," Philomena said bluntly.

Holly's eyes widened and her jaw dropped. She darted out of the room grabbing her cell phone hastily from Philomena.

"Ivy?" Holly said desperately on the phone while using her free arm to wriggle into her coat, still walking as quickly as her stilettos would permit.

"I think I just saw Jesus," Ivy moaned into the phone, while lying sprawled on Holly's couch.

"Are you sick?" Holly asked, pushing past a bloke on her way into an elevator. "What's happening?"

"My head's swimming," Ivy droned sickly. "Everything hurts. Do you believe in leprechauns and if so, is it possible that I have one dancing in my gut?"

"Did you ingest something that didn't agree with you?" Holly panted, bursting out of the elevator, into the large, hollow foyer at the building's entrance.

"I don't know," Ivy whined. "All I had today was that juice you left in the fridge."

"Juice is evil," Holly said, hailing a taxi outside. "Full of carbs. I would never keep such a thing in my fridge."

"I found like six jars," Ivy explained. "They smelled amazing. Figgy pudding. Cranberry jelly. Egg salad. Pumpkin pie. I've never drank pie before, so I chugged the whole thing."

"Oh my god!" Holly gasped, stealing a taxi from a ginger slam poet.

"They tasted kinda' off."

"Ivy, you drank my perfume samples!"

Ivy moaned so loudly the taxi driver gave Holly a peculiar glance.

"Ivy, don't go anywhere! I'm sending help! Do you hear me?"

There was no answer.

"Ivy?"

Holly frantically typed a phone number into her cell.

"Rex?" Holly nearly cried into the phone. "Rex, when you get this message, call me on my cell immediately. I need a list of every ingredient you put in the perfume samples. Specifically, the eggnog, pie, cranberry jelly and figgy pudding. It's an emergency!"

Holly's phone instantly rang.

"What!" Holly shrieked.

"Holly, it's me," Philomena said sheepishly on the phone. "What do I do with Brower and Port? They are hovering and making guttural noises."

"Keep them amused until I get back!"

"How?"

Holly hung up and fidgeted with panic.

"Can't you drive this thing faster?" she barked at the taxi driver.

"How?" the cabby sneered. "Every route is clogged."

Holly exhaled and tried another number on her phone again.

"Cash?" Holly said, cradling her cell between her chin and neck while she read a text on a different phone, "Ivy's been poisoned... No, I'm not joking. Rex literally just texted me and he said the perfume she drank doesn't contain anything that will kill her, but it does have extremely high alcohol content."

The taxi driver smirked.

"Please," Holly continued, "just be there with her. I don't know how long I'll be in this traffic."

***

Cash let himself into Holly's apartment, carrying several, paper grocery bags.

"Ivy?" he called.

Cash heard Ivy giddily singing a sloppy rendition of *Mele Kalikimaka* to herself on the couch. If slurring counts as singing.

"Are you okay?" Cash asked paternally. "Why are you making those noises?"

"Casherson?" Ivy slurred.

"How are you feeling, Sweetheart?"

"Sick," Ivy belched. "Buzzy. Queasy. Iffy. Wobbly. Horny. Are we alone? Where's Holly?"

"Stuck in a cab somewhere," Cash said, reaching into a paper bag. "Look what I got you from the bakery."

"Gingerbread men?" Ivy stuttered.

"Ginger settles your stomach."

Totally sloshed, Ivy lolled her eyeballs up at Cash adoringly.

"You are my hero," Ivy said.

"Whoa," Cash said, doing a doubletake when he noticed that Holly's Christmas tree was missing. In its stead stood a real spruce tree, adorned with homemade ornaments.

"Like it?" Ivy belched proudly. "I thought I'd surprise Holly."

"Holly is going to have a bird," Cash stated. "This is fantastic."

"You think?" Ivy said, pulling herself up to a sitting position on the couch. "It's like the one we had at the Spencers'."

"Who are the Spencers?"

"Holly never told you about the Spencers?"

"No."

"Probably didn't want you to know she's not all perfect and sparkly like you thought she was," Ivy giggled. "You're pretty."

"I don't get it," Cash squinted. "Who are the Spencers?"

"I'll never tell," Ivy sang, putting a silencing finger to her lips.

Cash looked almost in pain with curiosity.

"Those three years," Ivy said dreamily, "we was almost like a real family."

Ivy tried to get up but collapsed into Cash's arms.

"My legs are a little noodle-y," Ivy laughed.

"Ivy," Cash grunted, trying to prevent Ivy's limp body from slumping on the floor.

"You are such a stud," Ivy slurred.

"You are so drunk."

"Do you think Holly would mind if we went at it?"

"What in the world did you swallow?"

"Perfume," Ivy moaned. "Smell by breath. Figgy pudding. Sexy, right?"

Ivy stumbled, inadvertently pulling Cash to the ground. Finding themselves tangled on the couch, Ivy laughed at the ridiculous awkwardness, while Cash reddened and fumbled with his hands. After a series of cumbersome unraveling, Ivy somehow ended up on top of Cash. He swallowed hard, trying to find a way to maneuver his body out of this accidental entanglement. For a split moment, they looked into each other's eyes. As glassy as Ivy's eyes were, Cash briefly looked at her as though she was the most beautiful thing he had ever seen. Then he quickly averted eye contact.

"Dude," Ivy rasped, "I love you so damn much."

Drunk and lusty, and before Cash even had a moment to process, Ivy squished Cash's face between her hands and mashed a drunk, sloppy kiss on his mouth. Stunned, Cash writhed, having absolutely no idea where to put his hands.

When Holly made her aptly timed entrance, her look of genuine concern morphed into one of shock and horror.

Cash pulled himself out from under Ivy with the stealth of a slippery otter.

Ivy giggled incessantly.

"It's not what it looks like!" Cash said, wiping harlot-red lipstick from his face.

"Then I guess it didn't look like us sucking face," Ivy giggled.

"Oh my God," Holly said, looking ashen.

"Kitten…" Cash tried.

"Unless I poop in a box and happen to be licking my own butthole, *do NOT call me Kitten!*"

"If you'll only let me explain…"

"Literally every time I walk into this apartment, the two of you are engaged in a variety of shenanigans on my couch! I'm fed up with explanations!"

"I understand how you must feel…"

"Where is my tree?" Holly squeaked, her eyes literally bulging at the live tree in the corner.

"Mine's better," Ivy hiccupped. "You're welcome."

"Let me explain," Cash tremored. "I bought Ivy some comfort food, then she got all handsy…"

A knock at the door interrupted the ire-soaked silence in the room. When Holly answered, she discovered a very confused version of her neighbor Sid Broomer standing in the chevron-carpeted hallway.

"Sid?"

"Sorry to interrupt," Sid apologized. "I was just wondering if you have seen my Christmas tree? It disappeared from my apartment today. All the ornaments. Everything."

Frozen with horror, Holly slammed the door in Sid's face.

"*Really?*" Holly sneered at Ivy.

Ivy looked at Cash for support, but he could only shrug.

"Get out!" Holly barked at Ivy.

"Holly..." Ivy pleaded.

"You can't seriously hold this against her," Cash begged. "She's so ridiculously drunk. She lost control of her impulses."

"That's not a drunk thing. That's normal for her."

"You can't send her away in her condition! She can barely walk in a straight line!"

"I can't..." Ivy sniffled with tears welling in her eyes.

"I need to get out of here," Cash said, pursing his livid lips. "I can't look at you right now, Holly."

"Cash!" Holly gasped in disbelief.

"I mistook you for a compassionate, family-oriented woman. Clearly I was wrong. You can't be honest with me. You have a jealous streak I obviously didn't know about. The things you accuse me of! And now turning your underprivileged sister away right before Christmas! I need to leave before I say something I regret."

"Cash!" Holly shrieked. "That's not even fair! What do you expect me to think when the two of you are basically a pretzel on my couch every time I come home? I haven't worked a full day since she arrived. I keep having to come home and squelch a calamity!"

"She's family…"

"She's sabotaging my life! Today I had to leave in the middle of a meeting with Brower and Port! Why? Because this little vagrant drank my entire future!"

Cash squeezed his lips shut and nodded angrily.

"Cash," Holly said sheepishly. "I thought you were going to ask me to…"

"I changed my mind," Cash said haughtily as he stormed out of the apartment.

Holly turned to face Ivy with fury embossed on her face.

Ivy leaned backwards as though she was being blown backwards by a gale force wind.

"He was going to propose to me!" Holly spat at Ivy.

"I didn't know."

"Out!"

"Holly, you don't understand!"

"Get out!"

"You just can't kick me outa' here!"

"You are not my responsibility!"

"You just can't though!"

"Why not! You've ruined my life!"

"Because reasons!"

"Why!"

"Because I'm pregnant!" Ivy shrieked, immediately covering her mouth afterwards.

Shocked, all the anger oozed out of Holly, making her stand gaping for a moment.

"Oh my God," Holly said, sitting down. "You're going to *reproduce?*"

"I'm real scared."

"Of course you are, Hun. You can barely dress yourself."

"What am I going to do?" Ivy cried. "I have nowhere to live. I got no money. I don't know how to be pregnant."

"We'll figure something out."

"Does that mean that Poindexter and me can stay for good? And the baby?"

"I said we'll figure something out."

"Us three, we won't be no trouble. I promise."

"Who's the father?"

Ivy sheepishly shrugged.

"Oh, Ivy. You don't know?"

Holly noticed how vulnerable Ivy looked, curled up in a ball of shame.

"Is there anything you need?" Holly asked tentatively.

Ivy's face contorted into an ugly cry.

"Hun, please don't cry," Holly urged. "You look like a wet gerbil when you cry."

Ivy cried harder, heaving with each sob.

"So is there?" Holly asked again. "Anything you need?"

"A hug," Ivy said, barely audible.

Caught off guard, Holly awkwardly put her arm around Ivy.

Ivy hugged her back fervently, gripping Holly with a sense of throbbing urgency.

"We're going to figure this thing out," Holly choked.

CHAPTER TWELVE

Holly leaned in the bedroom doorway as she watched Ivy sleep with her ridiculous rat nestled into the pillow next to her head. Ivy looked so vulnerable lying there with a sticky strand of hair twined in her gaping mouth. There was a pathetic whistle each time Ivy exhaled in her sleep.

After gently closing the bedroom door, Holly rediscovered the present Ivy put under the tree. It was wrapped in paper towel with stupid mistletoe drawn on with a leachy sharpie marker. Unable to resist any longer, Holly opened the gift, finding a tattered photo album. Cracking the cover open, Holly swallowed a ball of emotion when she saw pictures of Holly and Ivy when they were little.

One photo depicted Holly pulling little Ivy through the snow in a wooden toboggan.

Another photo was of Holly putting the finishing touches on an immaculate snowman she had just built. Ivy, trying to copy Holly's snowman appeared to have built a pathetic sort of *snow wretch* and was looking rather disappointed with her failure.

The third photo told the story of Holly and Ivy as they stood outside a dilapidated apartment building. Holly had no coat on. Little, shivering Ivy was wearing her big sister's coat that was obviously too big for her.

On the next page was a photo of Holly and Ivy in a much nicer house, alongside a very wholesome looking couple. Although the home was decorated for Christmas, the little girls looked rather awkward, as though they did not know these people. If you were to look closely, you could see Holly squeezing little Ivy's hand tightly.

A snapshot captured little Holly and Ivy decorating a lush Christmas tree together. In this image, they looked happy and safe. A kind looking woman with wavy, chestnut hair was looking on with a tray of Christmas cookies.

Holly's eyes brimmed with tears as she mused on a picture of little Holly and Ivy making a mess a kitchen while making Christmas cookies together. Both girls along with the chestnut-haired woman were laughing wildly.

The final image made Holly's heart throb painfully. Holly and Ivy were cuddled up in a plaid blanket, sound asleep by a twinkling Christmas tree. They had their arms around each other as they smiled contentedly in their sleep.

Holly closed the book.

Her heart could not take anymore.

***

Sitting on his couch, Cash stared hollowly like a dismal sand tiger shark with tears on his face. He startled when there was a knock at the door. Quickly wiping tears away, he answered the door, finding Holly who was looking uncharacteristically contrite.

"When I said I needed time, I meant longer than seventy-five minutes."

"May I come in?" Holly asked sheepishly.

"I make a point of not inviting strangers into my home in the middle of the night."

Confused, Holly cocked her head.

"Who are the Spencers?" Cash blurted.

Holly lowered her head shamefully.

"Did you live with these people?" Cash interrogated. "Were you a foster kid or something?"

"See, I knew you would react this way if I told you."

"I'm reacting to the fact that you lied to me for two years! I don't even know who you are anymore! And to think I almost... What kind of a person hates her own sister?"

"Cash, I love you."

"Why?"

"Why? Because you're perfect."

"What else?"

"What more is there to be?"

"So if I wasn't perfect, if I didn't tick off all your little boxes..."

"What's wrong with striving for perfection? I thought that's why you loved me."

"Because you're *perfect?*" Cash cackled. "You're compulsive, neurotic, persnickety, pompous, impossible to please…"

"Are you saying I'm undeserving of love?"

"I loved you in spite of all those things! In a puppy-doggish way I used to find those things endearing."

"Loved? Used to?"

"I told you, I need time. Please go."

"When she kissed you," Holly practically squeaked, "did you like it?"

"Why would you ask me that?"

"You don't think I can see the way you look at her?"

"Of all the… Yes. If you want to know, I liked it. It was awesome. My lips could hardly believe their luck."

Holly's bottom lip trembled.

"I loved kissing Ivy because Ivy is a lot like you except…"

"What?" Holly quavered.

"She's fun," Cash shrugged.

Holly deflated.

"She's a hoot," Cash continued. "She's a firecracker. She's…"

"… pregnant."

"She's…?"

"Ivy is pregnant," Holly nodded. "She just told me."

"Who did this to her?"

"She doesn't even know, Cash."

"Oh my God."

"It's a good thing you like my sister so much because in a few months there's going to be two of her."

Holly turned to leave but hesitated.

"Or here's a cracker," Holly cried. "Why don't you marry her and the three of you can be a family. You know? The very thing you've never had?"

"That's not fair."

Holly slammed the door on the way out.

Cash kicked the door in frustration.

CHAPTER THIRTEEN
(FOUR DAYS BEFORE CHRISTMAS)

Emerging from the bedroom, bedraggled by a ruthless hangover, Ivy blinked what she thought was delirium from her eyes when she saw Holly unpacking shopping bags and organizing things methodically in the kitchen. Ivy winced with every clang, thud, rustle and clunk.

"Holly?" Ivy yawed like a Tonkinese cat.

Without breaking her stride, Holly handed Ivy a green, gloppy drink.

"Take," Holly instructed. "Drink. I'll break some bread."

"Are we taking holy communion?" Ivy winced.

"It's a hangover smoothie," Holly explained. "The bread is to neutralize your stomach acid."

"It's 4:00 a.m." Ivy pointed out.

"New York is always awake," Holly said, organizing things compulsively. "I've got a lot to do today and I need an early start. Thankfully, the stores never close…"

"What's all this?" Ivy asked, gesturing towards Holly's mysterious parcels.

"I went shopping," Holly said, taking items out of a bag. "Prenatal vitamins. A variety of dairy products. Classical womb music. Observe..."

Out of the bag, Holly grabbed the following items and lined them up systematically on the kitchen counter: pickles, olives, peanut butter, chocolate, eggs, bacon, spray cheese and sardines.

"I Googled the most common pregnancy cravings," Holly said crisply. "You're welcome."

Ivy peaked into a bag and found an adorable, baby outfit.

"Yes, well," Holly said awkwardly. "if I didn't step in you might let your child run around in a diaper until she's seven."

"All this is for me?" Ivy said with her voice raspy with humility.

"I certainly don't have any use for any of these things," Holly laughed nervously.

"You always did take good care of me," Ivy blinked.

"No more caffeine," Holly barked, trying to hide the emotion in her voice. "Don't inhale fumes. Avoid alcohol, pain killers, raw fish..."

"Guess that means you won't get to have your official Christmas Eve sushi."

Holly gaped.

"No festive pufferfish?" Holly asked, stung.

Ivy shrugged.

"Say, don't you have to work?" Ivy suddenly asked.

"It's Saturday," Holly said, averting eye contact. "I wouldn't be going in at all had it not been for this ridiculous deadline. Luckily there's no formal schedule on the weekends so I'll just have to work all night. No biggie."

"What about them guys?" Ivy asked obliviously. *"Bendown and Fart?"*

"Brower and Port," Holly corrected with extreme enunciation. "I don't meet with them until tomorrow. And yes, I do realize I will be paying for this with my soul, abandoning ship two days before deadline. I'll just have to make up for lost time tonight, tomorrow and the day after."

"You'd do that for me?"

"Someone needs to nurse your hangover," Holly sighed, barely believing her own altruism. "And keep that baby from coming out with two noses... Do you feel up to a little Christmas baking?"

"But this kitchen is immaculate like the blessed virgin."

"You think I'm afraid of a little flour?" Holly scoffed while opening a bag of flour.

Ivy goggled as flour poofed everywhere when Holly opened the bag, completely covering Holly with snowy whiteness. As Holly stood numbly, flour wafted all over the kitchen and spilled on the counter.

"Shut up," Holly snapped.

***

A platter of angel cookies adorned a sterling silver tray on the glass coffee table. Half of the angels were delicately frosted with pale pink icing, silver sprinkles dusting the perfectly smooth wings. The other half looked a little drunk and heavy-handed with the sprinkles. Glops of frosting were smeared unevenly and some of the angels were missing halos. Nonetheless, Ivy indiscriminately bit the head off every single angel, putting the decapitated seraphim back on the tray, much to the chagrin of Holly.

While watching a Christmas movie by the tree, Ivy was encased in a blanket taco while Holly sat with prim stiffness on the extreme opposite side of the couch. Her face contorted in revulsion when Ivy unexpectedly took a hard-boiled egg and scraped it into a bowl of leftover cookie frosting.

"Mmm," Ivy moaned. "Being pregnant is awesome. You should try this."

"You really need to return this tree to the Broomers," Holly said, changing the subject with a crinkled nose.

"Do we gotta?" Ivy pouted. "It's perfect."

"This tree is a lot of things," Holly said, angling her head critically. "Droopy. Anemic. *Stolen.* But perfect, it definitely isn't."

"Doesn't it remind you of the ones the Spencers used to get?" Ivy said, bounding on the couch like an excited toddler. "Remember when we used to make chain out of construction paper and reused those sticky candy canes from the year before..."

Uncomfortable, Holly quickly ate some frosting from her finger in the most demure way possible.

"How come you didn't tell Cash about the Spencers?"

Holly shrugged, still sucking the frosting from her finger.

"You ashamed of where we came from?"

"I don't *know* where I came from," Holly abruptly retaliated. "How do you tell that to a guy like Cash? Do you think he would give me the time of day if he knew about..."

"But he's more than just a rich stud muffin with yummy abs, smokin' arse and a smile that goes *'ting.'* Cash's got the biggest, squishiest heart of any guy I know. He woulda' understood."

"He's gone, Ivy. It's over."

"You don't know that for sure," Ivy persisted. "He just wants space. That don't mean..."

"He's pushing me away."

"But there's lots of reason's he might want space," Ivy grasped. "Maybe he's feverish. Or he suddenly developed one of them weird addictions like that lady on television who eats paper. He might not be ready to talk about that right now. Or maybe he's hiding a gnome in his apartment and wants to keep it a secret."

"Ivy, stop. He said he needs time to think."

"Again, lots of reasons for thinking."

"Don't."

"He could be thinking about the gnome."

"No."

"He could be thinking about how to surprise you for Christmas."

"Doubtful."

"Gasp! Maybe he's getting you a goat!"

"Ivy…"

"Ooo! I hope it's a goat!"

"Cash is not getting me a goat, Ivy! He's contemplating the notion of subtracting me from his life."

"Nah, that don't make sense."

"He thinks I lied to him. He thinks I mistreat you."

"Hey, that ain't true. You treat me real good."

"Right?"

"Better than the landlord of that basement I was squatting in that time. He was narsty. Say! Let's open presents!"

"It's not even Christmas Eve," Holly said, doing a doubletake from the sudden change of subject.

"No point of just sitting around, missing Cash," Ivy shrugged.

Excited, Ivy handed Holly a present, which had clearly been unwrapped already and carefully taped up again. Ivy did not seem to notice. Holly awkwardly opened the present, pretending that she had not already secretly opened it.

"It's…" Holly said, taking this opportunity to let the tears flow. "It's…"

"…all I have left of you," Ivy finished.

Holly thumbed through the pictures in the album as though she had not already done so.

"Do you remember when Mrs. Spencer used to turn all red when we called her *Mom?*" Ivy asked girlishly. "She'd say..."

"... "*I wish I was your mom. But if you call me that, I could get in trouble.*"

"Fact is," Ivy shrugged, "Mrs. Spencer was the closest thing we ever had to a mom. And any day of the week, Mr. Spencer could out-dad that stupid yob who disappeared when we was toddlers."

"They were pretty special," Holly said, discreetly wiping her nose. "It was the only time I can remember feeling truly safe."

"It was weird at first, though."

"Yep."

"I kept thinking they were up to something," Ivy recalled. "Like why are these weirdos so nice and crap? I thought for sure they had iffy intentions. Like that sketchy boyfriend Mom had that time. The one with the spider tattoo that covered his entire face? He seemed nice until he wanted to pretend we were lifelike puppets and used us to busk for cigarettes in the subway station. But the Spencers were nice for no reason. I wish I hadn't given them such a hard time at first."

"You were a child, Ivy. They understood."

"I feel kind of bad about peeing in all their houseplants," Ivy said, biting their lips. "Hiding their underpants. Clogging all the toilets with marshmallows..."

"Ivy, it wasn't your fault. You didn't have a cushy childhood," Holly reflected."

"You were the easy one for sure," Ivy nodded.

"No," Holly replied. "I was aloof and guarded to the point of being frigid for months after we first arrived. I didn't want to let my guard down... I'm sure that was even harder on them than unclogging the toilets."

"Sure wish they could have adopted us."

"Mom wouldn't let them," Holly sighed. "She never gave her consent."

"Why though?" Ivy inquired. "It's not as though she wanted to be a mom. But Mrs. Spencer..."

"She made the best soup."

"Right?"

"And that song she used to sing to you when you had nightmares?"

"She'd hold me practically all night sometimes, singing that to me. But I... I always felt safe as long as you were around, Holls. If it wasn't for you I'd probably still be hiding under a bed somewhere."

"Are...you sure you want me to have this book?" Holly asked. "It's so special to you."

"See, I don't know how long you'll let me stay here," Ivy quavered. "When I'm gone, I'll always remember you. But I'm scared that over time, while you're closing deals and getting famous, that I might waft right out of your mind forever. I don't think I could stand that."

Holly looked thoughtfully at Ivy for a beat.

"My turn?" Ivy bubbled.

Holly snapped out of it and handed Ivy her gift. As Ivy ripped off the paper in a frenzy, Holly craned her neck, curious about what Philomena had purchased for her sister. Inside the parcel was an extremely stylish jacket. Holly's eyes became wider than Ivy's.

"Holy frig!" Ivy yowled. "Feel how soft…"

"Genuine sheep skin?" Holly's voice wobbled with disbelief.

"I'll bet this cost more than the whole sheep!" Ivy chirped.

"Pretty close."

"It'll keep me so warm!" Ivy said, hugging the jacket childishly. "All them nights on the street. All them heating bills I can't pay. You must have put so much thought into this."

Holly hiccupped guiltily.

"There's even deep pockets for Poindexter! You thought of everything, Holls!"

Holly bit her lip to the point of nearly puncturing it.

***

Her left arm was already in her coat sleeve when Holly heard the sniffling and muffled sobs coming from her bedroom. Or Ivy's bedroom as it was now referred to by Ivy. With a heaving exhale and a swift glance at the clock on the microwave, Holly rapped on the bedroom door with her knuckle.

"Ivy? You okay in there?"

On the other side of the door, Ivy quickly stuffed stolen articles of clothing, which still had the tags, back into her duffel bag.

"Yeah," Ivy lied, wiping tears and snot from her face.

"Are you crying?" Holly asked, entering the room.

"No. I mean yes. The stupid baby keeps making me cry."

"Stupid? How could you say that about my niece?"

"Niece?" Ivy asked, cocking her head with genuine confusion.

"I have a sharp intuition about these things."

Ivy lowered her head.

"Look," Holly said, taking a seat on the bed. "I don't have a lot of time before work, but I should talk to you about something. I was thinking about the Spencers today. I haven't thought about them much before you arrived. I guess I wanted to just leave that part of my life behind me."

"I shouldn't o'interfered," Ivy apologized. "Things was great with you until I showed up."

"No," Holly said bluntly. "I was preoccupied with filling my life with busywork and compulsive detail. I wanted people to think I was a poised, professional. Bred and preened like a trained poodle."

"You are!" Ivy said earnestly. "Bred and preened. Not a poodle."

"Ivy, no. I'm exactly like you. Lost. Confused. Alone."

"What about Cash?"

"I'm not who he thought I was. He thought I was a distinguished executive. Now he knows I'm nothing but a common street urchin."

Troubled, Ivy opened her mouth to say something.

"Besides," Holly sighed. "he's in love with you."

Stunned, Ivy's eyes filled back up with tears.

"Nah," Ivy said.

"The irony? If I had just told him the truth about being uprooted from eleven foster homes... If I hadn't acted like an uppity... Maybe he would have married me. Maybe I'd have the family I always wanted.

Ivy stared agonizing at her duffel bag.

"I don't feel well," Ivy said, grabbing her duffel bag and bolting for the door.

"What are you doing? If you don't feel well, you should hop into bed and drink some evening primrose tea."

"The baby needs air," Ivy said as she scrambled out of the apartment, leaving Holly perplexed.

CHAPTER FOURTEEN

A cyclone of musings whirled through Holly's head as she trotted briskly past Philomena's desk: Brower and Port. How could she patch things up with Cash? Christmas was only two days away and she was running out of time to prepare. Brower and Port. Maybe there was hope for Ivy after all. Brower and Port. This would be the first Christmas in her adult life that she would not have Christmas Eve sushi next to her dazzlingly ivory tree. Was Cash really falling for her delinquent sister or was all the stress of the holiday season playing Boggle with her brain? Brower and Port. Ivy was knocked up and hopelessly inept. Would she drop the baby on its head? Forget to get it vaccinated? Put tequila in its bottle? Accidentally put it in the microwave? How did this even become Holly's problem? Could she salvage Christmas? Her relationship with Cash? Brower and freaking Port?

"You have like five messages," Philomena said, waving her hand in front of Holly to get her attention as she walked briskly past.

"No time."

"They tried calling you on your cell but…"

"I've got a lot on my mind here."

"I really think you should…"

"Mena, I just blew off the morning entertaining my impregnated sister. I need to make up for lost time."

"But this is serious," Philomena said seriously while wearing ridiculous reindeer antlers.

"Not as serious as my career," Holly unintentionally barked. "I need to pull an all-nighter if I'm going to make any headway here."

"But it's Saturday..."

"Crunch time knows no weekends. You know that."

"That's not what I mean."

"Please, no interruptions until I emerge from my office."

"Could you at least return this one message..."

"No."

"Holly, I really don't think you understand."

"I don't care who it was that left that message," Holly said with a heaving sigh while pinching the arch of her nose to alleviate the throbbing stress. "Call him back and tell him I'm unattainable for the next twelve to fifteen hours."

"Are you sure?"

"Mena!"

"Okay," Philomena mouthed as Holly slammed her office door. She sighed as she called Cash back. "Hey," she said on her cell phone, "it's Philomena calling you back from the office."

"Is she coming with me to the Christmas banquet or what?" Cash answered on the phone.

"I'm sorry, Cash. I tried."

"I don't believe this. Those tickets cost…"

"I know."

"This is rich. She was the one begging for another chance and then… Sorry, you probably don't want to hear about all this."

"Oh, but I do."

"It's kind of private."

"Are the two of you doing okay?"

"That's not something I should be discussing with my girlfriend's assistant. No offence."

"If there's anything I can do…"

"Thanks, Mena."

Cash hung up and Philomena stared helplessly at her phone.

***

With her duffel bag flung over her shoulder, Ivy skulked into a clothing store. Looking around to see if anyone was watching, she unzipped her bag, and discreetly rummaged around with one hand, scrounging for the articles of clothing she had previously stolen. Stealthily slipping behind a rack of fuzzy shrugs, Ivy was just about to pull a silk chemise out of her bag when her cell phone rang. Startled, she shoved the chemise back into the bag and zipped.

"Yep," Ivy said on the phone.

"Ivy?" Cash said on the phone.

"Casherson?" Ivy said, pretending to browse. "What's going on?"

"How are you feeling?"

"What?"

"Holly told me about the…"

"Oh. I guess I feel… knocked up."

"Are you busy?"

"Me? Nah. Just here returning Holly's Christmas present."

"Are you feeling up for a bit of fun tonight?"

"In what sense?"

"I'm sorry if this sounds a little forthcoming but I'm kind of in a bind and I didn't know who else to call."

"Hey man, you know I'd basically eat aluminum foil for you."

"Sure," Cash laughed nervously. "See, there's this banquet tonight. For my work…"

"Banquet?" Ivy asked, scrunching her nose. "What's that, like some kind of foot fest or whatever? If so, I'd love to help except I think feet are kind of gross. I'm sorry you had to find out this way."

"No, Ivy, no. Banquets have nothing to do with feet."

"But you said it was for your work. Aren't you the go-to foot guy?"

"I'm inviting you to a formal dinner with my colleagues. Gowns and tuxes. Dancing."

"Whoa, wait, stop the banana train. Shouldn't you be taking Holly to this shindig?"

"That was the plan," Cash exhaled.

"I don't think this is such a good idea, Casherson. Holly is your girl. Besides, I don't own a gown or a tux."

"Holly is not going."

"Is this because of the goat?"

"The... what?"

"Or are you guys legit on the rocks? Because I don't want to be no ho."

"Okay, look. Yes, I bought the ticket for Holly. Yes, we are squabbling but it's Christmas and I just thought... I tried to reach out to her and she blew me off. I'm in a sticky situation because these tickets were obscenely expensive..."

"I feel like I'd be making things worse if I go."

"You would be doing me an enormous favor."

"Are you sure though? Because this feels weird."

"I am quite literally begging you right now."

"I mean, it's tempting. I've never been to a cumquat before."

"Banquet."

"Will there be fries?"

"No."

"That's disappointing."

"So what's the verdict?"

"I'm not guilty unless the salesgirl catches me."

"What?"

"What?"

"Can I pick you up at 7:00?"

"What do I wear though?"

"Borrow something."

Ivy bit her lip as she eyeballed a sequin dress adorning a pretentious mannequin.

CHAPTER FIFTEEN

Cash locked arms with Ivy as they entered the sparkly, velvety banquet hall. Ivy goggled around the room at all the posh foot doctors as she scrunched the butt-fabric on her gown when it rode up. Her lip curled with curious revulsion when a gloved waiter walked by with a tray of salmon mousse blossoms and perfectly spherical bites of duck liver. She smiled stiffly at anyone who happened to walk by. Everyone smelled really good, and she had never seen so many champagne glasses, updos and judgmental looks in one room. The sparkle from the blingy necklaces on literally every woman's neck hurt Ivy's eyes. She blinked repeatedly to avoid temporary blindness.

"I feel like a fish stick without ketchup," Ivy said, leaning in confidentially to Cash.

"You look smashing," Cash reassured her.

"Everybody's looking at me."

"They obviously like your dress. Where did you get it?"

"I borrowed it like you told me."

"I've never seen Holly wear that dress before."

"I didn't borrow it from her. But don't worry. I left the tag on so I can sneak it back into the store tomorrow."

"Oh my god, you're so funny!" Cash said, misunderstanding.

Ivy smiled vacantly and blinked.

"Dr. Bartholomew!"

Cash turned to find an impossibly tall man with silver hair gelled meticulously into a Ken doll quiff. He was wearing an Armani suit and nursing a flute of Prosecco.

"Great to see you, Irving," Cash said, giving the man a firm handshake. "Ivy, this is Dr. Irving Petigru, head of podiatry at Mount Sinai."

"Pleasure," Irving said, extending his hand to Ivy.

Ivy gave Irving a fist bump, making her fingers flutter to simulate an explosion. "S'up, Doc?"

Cash pursed his lips with amusement.

"You found yourself quite a firecracker," Irving winked at Cash.

"You guys know Sleazy Joe Kaboom?" Ivy asked, her eyes popping with excitement. "He sells the best illicit explosives out of the trunk of his car."

"Ivy is Holly's sister."

"I'm just a stand-in," Ivy explained bluntly. "I'm not a whore or anything in case you were wondering."

"Looks like you're in for a fun evening," Irving said to Cash, gesturing to Ivy with his wine flute.

"I know it," Cash said, winking at Ivy.

"I think he dug me," Ivy said, craning her neck way too far while watching Irving Petigru slice through the crowd.

"Why wouldn't he?" Cash asked, eyeballing Ivy's dress.

"I 'unno. I feel a little like I'm in a fishbowl with everyone looking at me weird."

"You're a shiny, new penny. They're just curious. You don't have to feel self-conscious."

"These people look like they've totally got their shit together. Look at how springy that lady's hair is. I want to touch it."

"Please don't. Let's go find our seats."

***

Holly's eyeballs quivered as she stared at her computer screen, clacking furiously on the keys. She was barely aware of Philomena leaning into her office, pursing her holly berry glossed lips.

"I'm thinking maybe you should check your..."

"Not checking my messages, Mena," Holly said, stick clacking, still with quivering eyeballs.

"I know you're under a lot of pressure..."

"Got that right."

"And I understand that you've given me my marching orders..."

"Bye-bye."

"But as your friend…"

"Mena…"

"But it's Saturday."

"I am aware of the…"

"Saturday, December, twenty-one."

"Two days before deadline. Got it."

"It also happens to be the day of the Podiatry Banquet."

Holly instantly stopped clacking.

"You told Cash I couldn't go, right?"

"No."

"Mena! I specifically told you to…"

"How in the world could I tell Cash such a thing?" Philomena squeaked. "And why should I? This is between you and Cash. I'm not your go-between."

"So Cash thinks I'm going with him to the banquet?" Holly asked, yanking on her hair in angst.

"The banquet has already started so I assume he figured it out for himself."

"Mena, you have to call him and…"

"Look, I know the two of you are having some problems."

"Who told…"

"You need to talk to Cash."

"I obviously don't have time!"

"Then I can't be held responsible for what happens next."

"What do you mean?"

"You need to decide what your priorities are, Holly."

Holly repeatedly banged her head against her desk.

***

Cash pulled Ivy's chair out for her once they arrived at their designated table.

"What are you doing?" Ivy asked, her lip curling with confusion.

"Being a gentleman."

"Why though?"

"I'm just pulling your chair out, so you don't have to do it yourself."

"I don't get it."

"Manners," Cash smirked. "It's just manners."

"Okay," Ivy said, sitting tentatively. "This is new."

"We are seated at Dr. Ruddfecker's table," Cash observed. "He has a lot of influence in the medicinal foot ointment arena. They say he's the guy to impress."

"No pressure here," Ivy said, mashing a dinner roll in her mouth. "Hey look! We're seated next to this big-ass speaker! The bass is going to be epic! Can't wait to bust some moves, am I right?"

"Ivy," Cash said with a meaningful look.

"Huh?"

"Thanks."

"For what?" Ivy said with her mouth full of bread.

"For doing this for me."

"It's the least I could do since you've been so nice to me." Ivy replied, spitting a carraway seed onto the white tablecloth and grimacing. "People aren't usually nice to me. Plus, I don't think this'll be all that boring. Sure, foot doctors are not famous for their urge to party, but there's lots of things to look at and I just saw a dude that looks like a Jonas brother. Also, what's a crostini? Some guy offered me one. Is it some kind of holistic joint? I don't think I want one."

"I'm so glad you're here," Cash said, squeezing Ivy's hand. "This'll be fun."

Ivy pinkened.

"Look who the cat dragged in!" a booming voice bellowed heartily as he sat his rotund self on a skirted conference chair. He rubbed his hands together and instantly took two dinner rolls from a basket on the table, along with a fistful of mini-butters.

"Is he talking about me?" Ivy whispered to Cash as she stiffened into a plank. "It's my stupid hair, isn't it. I knew I should have showered before I came here. Jaysus, now I'm self-conscious. Smell my pits."

"He was talking about me," Cash chortled. "You smell fine, just have fun."

"But what if I embarrass you in front of the ointment guy?"

"You won't."

"I'm not really like any of these other broads here. With their boingy hair, impulse control and their lipstick that matches. Do they ALL have British accents because that's definitely how it feels."

"New arm candy, Bartholomew?" Ruddfecker asked, jerking his head towards Ivy and putting a linen napkin in his collar.

"Dr. Ruddfecker, this is Ivy."

"Ugh!" Ruddfecker barked unintentionally. His voice did not seem to have a volume control. "Don't talk to me about Ivy. I've got the stuff sprawling all over my English cottage in Cheshire. Can't control the infernal plant. And it attracts ants."

"I mean sometimes they called me Archie at the group home," Ivy piped up. "Short for *The Archfiend of the Duplicitous Spiders*. But they were mostly high so..."

Ruddfecker paused for a moment before bursting into a fit of laughter, spewing crumbs unintentionally from his mouth. "That," Ruddfecker said, wagging a finger at Ivy, "is funny. Hey, Dr. Agnew," Ruddfecker said to a stiff, aristocratic man finding his seat at the table, "you have to meet Archie here. Bartholomew brought her." Ruddfecker was still bouncing in his seat from laughter.

"Charmed," Agnew said aloofly, offering Ivy a limp handshake. A plastic woman who resembled a mannequin in a Rue de Passy fashion boutique loomed behind him.

"It's Ivy actually," Ivy said. "Nobody's called me Archie since I was detained for trying to snuff sidewalk chalk."

"*Dr.* Marvin Agnew," Agnew said, enunciating his title as though he was not literally one of hundreds of doctors in the room. "And this is my mistress, Mary."

"Are you quite contrary?" Ivy eagerly asked the plastic woman. "And if so, how does your garden grow?"

Mary raised her eyebrows in shock. Although nobody could tell because of her elaborate Botox therapy. Nonetheless, Agnew pulled a chair out for her and she took thirty-five solid seconds to sit down in her ridiculously tight pencil dress.

"Isn't Archie a scream?" Ruddfecker guffawed, slapping Agnew playfully with the back of his hand. "She's a hell of a lot more fun than that uptight bird Cash brought to the banquet last year."

Cash choked on his water.

"She is a barrel of monkeys," Agnew said aloofly, wiping Ruddfecker's imaginary germs from his tux sleeve.

"Why does he talk like that?" Ivy asked of Agnew as though he wasn't sitting right across the table from her. "He talks like a boring cartoon villain. Does he mean to?"

Ruddfecker exploded with laughter, so much so that the entire table bounced with rattling cutlery and jiggling water glasses.

"I am a foot surgeon," Angew said aloofly, adjusting his pretentious bow tie. "Which basically makes me an oligarch, but not in Aristotelian terms."

"So foot surgeons ALL talk like that?" Ivy asked, cocking her head. "With fake, snooty accents and whatever? That's wild. Do you all have to take a special class or…"

Mistress Mary hiccupped with an accidental giggle but washed it down with a demure sip of water.

"She called it," Ruddfecker laughed, again flapping the back of his hand on Agnew's tux sleeve, as his eyeballs lolled disapprovingly at Ruddfecker.

"I fail to see…" Agnew began.

"You are such a snob!" Ruddfecker squeaked with laughter, dabbing his eyes. "So much so that it's quite hilarious. I love how Archie here just blurted it out like that. Classic!"

"This is blatantly disrespectful," Agnew said, puffing himself up and enunciating in an even more precise accent. "given the influence I have in the foot empire."

"And yet they say that *I'm* the guy to impress," laughed Ruddfecker. "Go figure."

"Stay in your lane, Ointment Boy," Agnew snarled.

"That's big talk from a guy who manipulates people into surgery when an ointment will do the trick."

"Don't be preposterous," Agnew intentionally spat. "Foot surgery is a high art. Unlike you and your pseudoscientific witchcraft…"

"I've got an ointment for everything," Ruddfecker bragged. "Literally. In fact, I'm working on a multi-purpose emollient that will make most foot surgeries obsolete in five to ten years. Only eight dollars a jar. I have samples in my satchel if anyone wants to try."

"You wouldn't dare," Agnew said with his eyes flaring.

"This guy though!" Ruddfecker laughed, pointing at Angew with his thumb. "'*You wouldn't dare!*' Oh my gosh, you're such a turd. Tell him, Archie."

"I'm still trying to figure out why his spine doesn't bend," Ivy said. "Like at all. Did he leave the hanger in his shirt?"

The table bounced and rattled again from Ruddfecker's laughter.

Mistress Mary hid a twitter of laughter behind her linen napkin.

Cash snorted from an impulsive chuckle.

"Well then," Agnew said, adjusting himself, "it seems they've served dinner. Perhaps it will make it harder to roast the most influential person at the table when your mouths are stuffed with Dungeness crab with eelgrass garnish."

Ivy's eyes widened as a plate was plunked down in front of her. A large crab was staring back at her from the plate. With eyes.

"What is that?" Ivy asked, stiffening and leaning back as though the crab might lunge at her with its pincers.

"Crab," Cash said, stuffing a napkin in his collar.

"Don't worry," Ivy said, unzipping a stolen handbag. "I brought fries in my purse."

"Wait," Angew said, perking up eagerly, "are those fries?"

CHAPTER SIXTEEN

With a sudden bout of restless leg syndrome, Holly listened to the missed messages on her phone.

"Holly, it's Cash. Look, I know things are weird with us right now and this probably isn't the time to remind you, but the banquet is tonight. You have the date in your phone, right? I need to pick you up no later than 7:00 so call me back as soon as you get this message, okay?"

Beep.

"Cash here. Did you get my message? Check your messages and call me back. It's important. Ciao."

Beep.

"Hey, it's me again. Did you get tied up at work? Are you in the zone or something? I really need you to call me back. It's urgent. K. Bye."

Beep.

"Okay, now I'm getting worried. I have to attend this event tonight and I can't exactly get a refund when the proceeds have already been invested in a worthy cause. I know your deadline is coming up, but PLEASE. Call me back."

Beep.

"Please tell me you're not blowing me off because of the spat. Look, I know it'll be awkward tonight, but you always feel awkward at these things anyway. Okay, that wasn't a great sell. But still. I need you to call me presently... Wait, presently?"

Beep.

"Holly. I know I said some things. I was hurt. Shocked. Disappointed. Confused. But I don't know if I'm ready to give up on you. I thought maybe... (loud exhale)... we could finally have a chance to reconnect tonight at the banquet. Have some alone time. If this is something that you want, then PLEASE call me back."

Beep.

"Holly. Kitten. Did you forget? Or is this it? I need to know... Call me."

Beep.

"Holly, if you don't call me back, I'm going to have to assume it's over."

Beep.

"Okay. Going without you."

Beep.

Holly frantically flapped around her desk, causing loose sheets of paper to fly around in a flurry while screaming for Philomena.

"What's going on in here?" Philomena asked, popping he head in the doorway.

"Where's my phone!" Holly said, flustered. "I have to find my phone!"

"In your hand."

"In my..." Holly discovered her cell phone in her hand – the same place it had been while she was listening to Cash's messages. "I have to get in touch with Cash or everything will be ruined!"

"I'd say I told you so, but I'm not a jerk."

"What kind of a sociopath plans a party four days before Christmas anyhow?" Holly asked while calling Cash. "Oh my God. My entire world is about to crash in on me... why isn't he answering?"

***

"And that's how I got the weird scar on my groin," Ivy shrugged as everyone at the table laughed heartily, while all sharing fries from Ivy's purse.

"I must say," Agnew said after having somehow shed his haughty façade like an itchy blanket, "I've never quite met anyone who can lose consciousness on purpose."

"I guess I'm like one of them fainting goats," Ivy shrugged modestly. "It comes in handy when you want to avoid your social worker. Also the winos who pestered me when I lived in that pizza box fort for like a month. Hey, Mistress Mary, can I touch your hair?"

"Oh my goodness," Mistress Mary said giddily while leaning in towards Ivy, "I was hoping someone would ask. Go ahead!"

"That's so freaky," Ivy said, poking Mary's updo. "It doesn't move like at all."

Everybody laughed jovially.

"Archie, would you like anything from the bar?" Ruddfecker asked while dabbing a tear of hilarity from his eye.

"Whoa, ya, no. I'm..." Ivy said, indelicately miming pregnancy.

"I could get you a virgin daiquiri," Cash said confidentially, squeezing Ivy's hand.

Ivy's lips farted with an explosion of laughter. "You said it!"

"What?" Cash asked, half-laughing.

"VIRGIN!" Ivy squawked way too loudly in the throes of uncontainable laughter. "He said virgin!"

The table erupted with laughter.

"You did in fact say that," Ruddfecker howled. "Classic!"

"I say!" Agnew said, cramping from laughter.

Pinkening, Cash laughed too, putting a reassuring hand on Ivy's shoulder. "I'll be back soon," he assured her.

"So how long have the two of you..." Ruddfecker asked.

"Huh?" Ivy said, suddenly realizing that she was gazing stupidly at Cash as he walked towards the bar. "Oh, the two of us? Like Cash and me? We're not..."

"You're not together?"

"Not in the eyes of the Lord, no," Ivy said, fervently shaking her head. "I ain't religious or nothing but we still don't pork. Oh crap. Can I say pork at a banquet? My sister doesn't allow it in her living room."

Everyone laughed and competed for the last remaining fries in Ivy's purse.

"Are you sure though?" Ruddfecker asked, mowing down on a fry.

"About what?" Ivy asked, clearing her throat for no reason.

"The way he looks at you..."

"Oh! You mean with his eyes?" Ivy laughed nervously while pointing at her own eyes. "You misunderstood. See, that's how he looks at people he feels sorry for."

"Why in the world would he feel sorry for you?" Angew asked, genuinely dumbfounded. "You are so colorful."

"Good word, colorful," Ruddfecker nodded.

"So refreshing," Agnew continued. "So honest, fun, unpretentious, witty and... oh darn it. What's the word I'm looking for, Ruddfecker?"

"Authentic."

"That's the one!"

Ivy swallowed hard. "That's awful swell of you to say, fellas," she said. "But the thing is... Like the thing with Cash and me..."

When Cash's phone rang with Holly's signature ring, Ivy seized this opportunity to grapple around in the pockets of Cash's suit jacket which was hanging on his chair. She took the liberty to answer it.

"Casherson's phone," Ivy said on the phone.

"Ivy?" Holly said on the phone with a squeak of ire.

"Hey, Sis. What can I do you for?"

"What are you doing answering Cash's phone?" Holly asked through clenched teeth.

"See," Ivy answered, twiddling her hair, "Cash woulda' answered the phone, except that he's at the bar trying to find a virgin."

"Where are you right now?" Holly barked.

"At... the banquet."

"He took YOU?"

"You was working."

"How could you do this to me?"

"I didn't do nothing," Ivy insisted. "I just got asked and before I knew it, I was talking about my groin, touching people's hair and getting free samples from this ointment guy. It's so cool, he just opened his bag and started piling all these little jars into my purse. It's just like getting stuff from the underground market except it's legal."

"You are going to ruin everything!"

"Again?"

"Get out of that banquet venue. Now."

"But Cash is my ride. And everyone here likes me."

"How is that possible?"

"Holly, I'm having fun. Please, can I stay?... Holly? Hello?"

***

"Philomena!" Holly shrieked in mid-stride with one arm already in her coat sleeve. "Call Victor, Cheyenne, Mel, Carl, Liz and Horatio into the office. That should about cover the work I was doing. I'd call them myself by I don't have that kind of time."

"You want me to *delegate?*" Philomena asked in a state of genuine shock. "You? Two days before deadline?"

"Do I look like a person who has a lot of options right now?" Holly asked while frantically trying to find her hand inside her coat sleeve.

"I thought you were pulling an all-nighter?" Philomena pointed out. "Only a few minutes ago you dug your little heels in..."

"Cash took Ivy to the banquet."

"Oh."

"This is a calamity. I have to get to the banquet venue before Ivy botches everything, but not before I squeeze into my chartreuse dress, reapply my makeup, do my hair up in a French roll and glue some lashes onto my eyelids. That doesn't leave me a lot of time to hail a cab and paint my nails on the way there."

"Do you even have time to do all that?" Philomena asked. "This being a calamity and all?"

"Honestly, Mena," Holly said, stepping into the elevator after pressing the button two hundred consecutive times. "People can't see me with my real eyelashes. What would they think?"

CHAPTER SEVENTEEN

Ivy indelicately slurped what was left of her virgin daiquiri through a straw while Cash mingled with an idiopathic plantar fasciitis specialist. Her eyeballs swerved over to the dance floor where Agnew was slow dancing with Mistress Mary and her unyielding hair. Meanwhile, Ruddfecker was blissfully handing out emollient samples to everyone in the room.

When Cash finished his conversation with a firm handshake, he coaxed Ivy on to the dance floor. She hesitated but Cash was nothing if not persuasive. Ivy had clearly never slow danced in her life so she was oblivious as to where she should put her hands. Cash clasped one of her hands and his and settled the other on the small of her back. She stepped on his shiny shoes a few times but eventually found her groove.

"You look good," Cash nudged. The smear of orange lipstick on her front teeth did not seem to bother him.

"I don't know."

"You really saved my butt tonight."

"Awe."

"I mean it, Ivy. You're a really good friend."

Ivy pursed her lips and looked away.

"Are you having a good time?"

"The best!" Ivy bubbled. "Have you been to the john? They put the toilet paper in baskets and the floors aren't sticky like the cans in Grand Central Station. It's like people don't even pee on the floor here. Mind. Blown."

"That's actually good to know," Cash gleamed good-naturedly. "I hadn't really thought about that before, but I suppose I was just taking the johns for granted."

"I feel like a freaking princess right now," Ivy said with her eyeballs bulging at all the stimuli around her. "I've never dressed up before and the food here tasted like... well, food. It's like crashing a wedding, except I was invited this time and I don't have to outrun a security guard with a baked potato in each hand and my mouth stuffed with carrot cake. This is literally the best Christmas I've ever had in my whole life and Christmas isn't even here yet."

"It really doesn't take a lot to make you happy, does it, Ivy?" Cash asked, putting a stray strand of hair behind Ivy's ear.

Ivy shrugged.

Cash pondered.

"This isn't exactly how I thought I'd be spending the holidays."

"Surprise!"

"Can... I tell you something?"

"I'm all ears."

"I have these airline tickets for Christmas Eve."

"You going somewhere?"

"Prague. I figured there's no reason for me to spend Christmas alone in my apartment."

"What?" Ivy asked, squinting and shaking her head interrogatively.

"I mean obviously the plan was initially to take Holly with me."

"What do you mean *was?*"

"I was going to whisk her away to Prague. You know, spontaneously."

"Holly? Spontaneous?"

"That was the glitch, yes. I had hoped to propose to her in Prague. But she had other plans."

"Sorry."

"It's not your fault. I didn't splurge for flight insurance so here I am with these two tickets to Prague. And things being on the outs with Holly…"

"Wait, what?"

"She made it clear she didn't want to work things out with me."

"But…"

"I left her scads of messages. I told her that if she wanted to give things another go, that we could try to reconnect at the banquet tonight. But she ghosted me."

"I don't think that's what she…"

"Do you want to come with?"

"Where?"

"To Prague."

"What, me? I don't even know what a Prague is."

"It could be nice."

"Nah. Holly…"

"Just as friends. No strings. I hate travelling alone."

"Holly's my sister though."

"Holly made it clear she didn't want to go."

"That's just 'cuz…"

"And I don't want to go with her anymore."

"Why though? She's your girl."

"She's not the person I thought she was."

"But she is…"

"Please consider this, Ivy. Think of it as a Christmas gift."

"You already gave me the furry muffs…"

"It'll be totally innocent. We'll get adjoining rooms."

"It ain't right."

"Prague is pretty this time of year," Cash urged. "I went in college. It would be nice to have some company. Come on, Ivy. I like you."

Ivy burst into tears.

"Ivy?" Cash said, wiping a tear from Ivy's face with his thumb.

"This is just too much," Ivy wept.

"I don't want you to cry. I just want..."

"I was always in trouble," Ivy sobbed. "Pickpocketing. Rude graffiti. Glue."

"What?"

"When Holly turned eighteen," Ivy said, catching her breath, "she took care of me. She worked at like six grocery stores trying to keep me in school. We lived in this scary building with a freaky smell and a guy upstairs who talked to his radiator."

"Calm down, Honey," Cash coaxed. "The baby..."

"I lied a lot," Ivy sniffled. "Ran with bad kids. The police was always showing up at Holly's door. I can't count how many bail dollars she forked over."

Cash hugged Ivy and held her for a lingering moment.

"Then one time," Ivy snuffed, "Holly didn't show up with the bail. I was on my own after that. Guess Holly had enough. Can't really blame her though."

"Why are you telling me this?"

"I don't deserve Prague, whatever the heck that is. I don't deserve all your niceness."

"Ivy..."

"Holly's real decent," Ivy said earnestly. "You guys is supposed to be together."

"I don't think so."

"But you guys is so cute, with your trendy haircuts and your expensive coffees. Your babies would be so smart."

"She was mean to you."

"She had her reasons. You don't know me the way Holly does. Then I show up with a duffel full of issues…"

"Her priorities…"

"You don't know how hard she had to work to dig her way out o' where we came from."

"She lied…"

"But…"

"HOLD IT RIGHT THERE!" Holly shrieked as she trotted dominantly into the room. Hundreds of heads turned, and the music screeched to a stop. Her ankle twisted on her stiletto a few times as she sliced her way through the crowd on her way to the dance floor. But Holly did not care.

"Holly…" Cash began.

"This is a betrayal!" Holly said, pointing back and forth between Ivy and Cash. "Is this what you do every time I work late? Get freaky in front of a plethora of podiatrists? To an Everly Brothers song no less? These," Holly said, gesturing to the hundreds of gawkers around them, "are people I was supposed to make a good impression on! To advance Cash's career! That is literally what girlfriends are for!"

"You blew me off," Cash reminded her.

"Don't take it personally," Holly said, waving his comment away with her partially wet fingernails. "I blew everybody off today. It had nothing to do with you, Cash."

"Holly, I..." Ivy tried.

"You!" Holly said, swirling around to face her sister. "Where did you get that dress!" she barked. "And where can I obtain one also!"

"Cash was in a pinch," Ivy explained. "I thought I was helping..."

"By leading every foot professional in New York City to believe that my man is cheating on me with a vagrant?"

"It's totally okay!" Ivy piped up. "I told everyone in this room that I am not a tart so don't worry."

"I can't believe I let my guard down," Holly said, laughing manically at the ceiling. "And then you just went ahead and sucked me in. Again! You always do this to me, Ivy! I just never learn!"

"Holly, I was just tryin'a..."

"Why did you have to botch my perfect Christmas?" Holly squeaked with emotion.

Ivy's bottom lip quivered.

"Let's go, Ivy," Cash said, pulling Ivy out of the room.

"Cash!" Holly called. "Oh come ON!"

CHAPTER EIGHTEEN
(THREE DAYS BEFORE CHRISTMAS)

Curled in a ball on her couch, hugging a festive, snowflake throw cushion, Holly stared at the door with bulging, tired eyes. Ivy did not come home after the banquet and Holly had nearly hugged the stuffing out of the cushion waiting for her.

"This should not be my problem," Holly confessed to a ridiculous elf decoration hanging on her stolen Christmas tree. "Worrying about a shameless miscreant who has zero survival instincts. I absolved myself of this responsibility a long time ago... And yet here she is, sucking me right back in. She has done nothing but hold me back. I should not be sitting here the day before a deadline, staring at the door like a cocker spaniel, waiting for her to come home. Why does this even matter to me? Why do I have to care so much about her? She's a twat... Don't look at me that way, you pointy-hatted hobgoblin."

Holly gasped when the door squeaked open. Ivy tip-toed cartoonishly into the apartment with long, exaggerated strides.

"Ehem," Holly said, pretending to clear her throat.

Ivy stopped in mid-exaggerated stride.

"Where were you all night?" Holly asked, tossing the throw cushion to provide a visual demonstration of her aggravation.

"See…"

"Why do you look like that?"

"I'm pretty sure this is what I've always looked like," Ivy shrugged.

"I mean why is your hair disheveled and why is your dress on inside out? And why is the tag still on your dress? And not to belabor the point, but *where were you all night?*"

"Whoa, okay," Ivy said, shaking her head to make sense of all the questions. "I was at Casherson's place and I look like this because…"

"I don't want to know," Holly moaned, holding her head.

"Then why did you ask?"

"What made you think it was a good idea to spend the night with Cash?"

"He invited me."

"And you went along with it?"

"He had chips."

"At no point of time, did you think to yourself, *'hmm. Maybe it's a tad inappropriate to spend the night with my sister's serious boyfriend?'*"

"I didn't think it was safe to come back here, what with you flipping your lid at the shindig last night."

"This is so many different levels of wrong!"

"We didn't shag or nothing, honest! We just talked and crap."

"You expect me to believe that? When you tippy-toe into my apartment looking like a shameless tart?"

"I swear I didn't shag Cash!"

Holly exhaled.

"I shagged the Uber driver on the way home," Ivy shrugged. "His name was Art. Nice guy."

"Ivy!"

"What?" Ivy practically whined. "It's not like I can get any pregnant-er!"

"Ivy, this is why you keep getting yourself into trouble!" Holly squeaked with emotion. "I can't keep swooping in and fixing things every time..."

"Why are you being so uptight about this?" Ivy squeaked back. "Art and I is grownups. Plus we only did it for like six minutes and he wasn't even that good at it so it didn't count. I thought you'd be proud of me for not sleeping with Cash. Now my feelings are hurt."

"It would be remiss of me not to ask what you and Cash *talked* about into the wee hours."

"Huh?"

"You talked to Cash literally all night," Holly repeated, clenching. "What. Did. You. Talk. ABOUT?"

"That's kind of private, isn't it?"

"Do you realize I've been waiting up all night *worrying...*"

"Alright, alright, alright already," Ivy said, waving her hands around as though she was shooing away mosquitos. "We talked about me."

"You?"

"And also him."

"Him?"

"Uh-huh."

"You and him?"

"That's what I said, yes."

"As in *you and him?*"

"You like to say that."

"What do you mean, *you and him?*"

"Like," Ivy blinked, "there's Ivy. That's me. And then Cash, who is... well, you know who Cash is..."

"How are you this stupid?"

"What?"

"Are the two of you together?"

"He's at his place."

"*Together!* Stop pretending you don't know what I mean!"

"I don't know what you're accusing me of, but it wasn't my fault this time."

"Can you please just tell me what you were talking about, all cozied up on his leather couch for the entire duration of the night?"

"It's a secret though. I don't think I can say."

Holly bit her throw cushion so hard, it tore open.

"But I didn't do nothing wrong," Ivy promised with wide eyes. "I promise. I wouldn't do nothing to hurt you, Holly. You gotta' believe me."

"Ivy…"

"And I really did do it with the Uber guy," Ivy said earnestly. "I'm sure my DNA is all over his car if you want to involve the Feds."

"I don't want to involve the Feds," Holly muttered.

"Golly, that's swell."

"I guess I'm glad you're not dead," Holly muttered even more resentfully.

"For reals?" Ivy said, with tearfully shimmering eyeballs. "That's literally the nicest thing you or anyone else has ever said to me."

"Can you at least tell me why Cash took you to the banquet?"

"You was working and blowing off all o' Casherson's messages."

"So Cash did this out of spite. Is that what you're saying?"

"More like he was desperate on account of you standing him up at the last minute. Do you know how much those tickets cost? Holy cow!"

"That's offensive."

"Did I take the cow's name in vain?"

"First of all, Cash knew about my deadline so he should not have taken this as personally as he did. And you knew that he and I were in a delicate situation. How could you literally go on a date with a man with whom I'm struggling to stay in a relationship?"

"I thought I was doing you a solid. Kind of covering for you while you was at the office, sniffing people."

"That's not what I..."

Holly groaned from exasperation when her cell phone rang.

"What is it, Mena?" Holly said on the phone.

"Where are you?" Philomena asked on the phone.

"At home. Why?"

"Brower and Port have been waiting for you for the past thirty-five minutes."

"But the deadline's not until tomorrow."

"We need to have the product on the shelves tomorrow," Philomena corrected. "Today is the day we get emergency approval to meet that goal."

"WHAT!"

"You're on your way, right?" Philomena said nervously. "Holly, please tell me you're on your way."

"I'm a literal train wreck!" Holly squawked as she looked at her red, glassy eyes and staticky hair in the mirror. "I've been waiting up all night for my reprobate sister to arrive home!"

"Oh that's not good."

"Get Victor. Cheyenne…"

"It's Sunday," Philomena apologized. "And three days before Christmas. I'll never be able to convince everyone to come in today. Especially since the lot of them worked until well after 4:00 a.m. covering for you last night."

"What about Anuj?"

"You sent him to Yazoo City. Holly, you told me to arrange his trip last week."

"Sweet Baby Jesus in the manger!" Holly swore as she struggled to pull on her boots.

"Hurry, Holly," Philomena begged. "Brower just made a gurgling noise. I don't know what that means."

"On it!" Holly shrieked.

"Where are you going?" Ivy asked.

"Work."

"Shouldn't you get dressed or something?"

"Shut your gob, Ivy!" Holly barked as she darted out the door with her coat half-on.

***

As she stumbled cumbersomely out of the elevator Holly realized she was wearing one black boot and one red boot. Out of breath she fumbled towards Philomena's desk, where a terrifying nutcracker glared at Holly judgmentally with his painted-on eyes. Philomena's jaw dropped when she beheld Holly wearing last night's dress and pantyhose with a conspicuous rip. One of Holly's false eyelashes was becoming unglued, resembling a meandering spider. Staticky hair escaped wildly from her partially dismantled French roll with bobby pins poking out every which way.

"Whoa," Philomena said speechlessly.

"Are they still here?" Holly said breathlessly while tussling with her coat that stubbornly refused to let go of her arm.

"They're in your office," Philomena replied, cocking her head at Holly's disheveled self.

"I can fix this," Holly said, raising an index finger. "I always fix things."

"Adda girl?" Philomena said feebly as Holly fumbled into her office.

***

Brower and Port simultaneously swerved around in their swivel chairs when Holly toppled clumsily into the room, trying to hide one mismatched boot behind the other before she took a seat. Their eyebrows triangulated when Holly cleared her throat much too loudly and made a futile attempt to primp her sagging updo.

"Sorry to keep you waiting," Holly hiccupped. "Now. Who's excited for the new fragrance?"

"We've been waiting for an unseemly amount of time."

"Understood," Holly said with faux confidence while indiscreetly hiding her bra strap back under her dress. "But I assure you that when we deliver this superior product, it will all be well worth the wait."

"Where's the nog?" Port asked bluntly.

"I've been in communication with the lab...," Holly said, pretending to rifle through random papers.

"So have we," Port continued. "Rex said there's been an unforeseen obstacle. What did he mean by that?"

"I don't know offhand," Holly admitted. "I do know that the lab was working well past 4:00 a.m..."

"And where were you?" Brower burbled.

"Excuse me?" Holly asked, blinking profusely from the loosening false eyelash.

"Where were you, Miss Plover, the night before deadline?" Brower barked. "When the lab confirmed that the formula was deemed incompatible with human skin? When the rest of your team was busting their ass trying to nonetheless deliver the product in a timely fashion? *Where were you?*"

"I... I had a family emergency," Holly swallowed.

"Again?"

"It was unavoidable," Holly persisted. "If it was humanly possible for me to be there..."

"This is unacceptable," Port said in disgust.

"I delegated at least five people to cover for me," Holly said, blinking back tears. "I did everything I could to…"

"None of those delegates had the authority or the knowledge to advise the laboratory," Port berated. "You spearheaded this project and then abandoned ship at the precise moment you were needed. And now here we are, on the day we were supposed to secure emergency approval…"

"Who the hell would buy eggnog scented perfume anyway?" Holly squeaked emotionally. "You asked us to defy the laws of chemistry in a completely unreasonable amount of time! Right before Christmas, no less! You set us up for failure and I don't see it's fair how you are pinning this on me!"

"You can't absolve yourself of responsibility…"

"I told you I had a family emergency!"

"A family emergency?" Brower smirked, eyeballing Holly's tousled attire. "Is that why you look as though you've been carousing the night away?"

Holly swallowed audibly. "My baby sister didn't come home last night."

"Look me in the face and explain to me why that is our problem."

"Sirs…"

"We're done," Port said abruptly. "Destroy the contract. This whole thing is…"

"Mr. Port…"

"Your ineptitude is a disgrace, and we refuse to work with…"

"But I pulled lemurs out of my butt-crack for you!" shrieked Holly.

"I beg your pardon?"

"I agreed to your asinine terms!" Holly continued. "I frazzled my lab techs! I forfeited my perfect Christmas and lost a solid week's worth of sleep! And for what? So you could plump your egos with a gimmicky idea that nobody would even go for anyway! On the shelf on the twenty-third of December? What's the point of that even?"

"Ms. Plover, this is unseemly."

"I'll tell you what's unseemly," Holly seethed. "The fact that I sold my soul to a couple of daft numb-nuts with virtually no sense of smell!"

The eyes of Brower and Port simultaneously turned into slits of ire.

CHAPTER NINETEEN

Holly did not even have the energy to slam the door when she arrived home. She just sort of wafted in, shed her coat to the floor and shuffled into the apartment, merely existing. Ivy, on the other hand was wearing nothing but an apron and oven mitts, frittering with something or other in the kitchenette.

"Holls!" Ivy bubbled as she scraped some incinerated cookies from a pan with a partially melted spatula. "I burned you some shortbread angels. Want some?"

"Why aren't you wearing pants?" Holly asked lifelessly.

"Didn't want to get my borrowed dress dirty while I was baking," Don't worry though. Although you can't tell by looking at me, I'm wearing your pretty lady jammies under this here apron."

"Can you just yell at yourself for being an idiot?" Holly said defeatedly. "I just don't have the energy."

"Hey," Ivy said, raising an index finger. "I just noticed something. You're not at work."

"A very astute observation," Holly said dully.

"Why though? I thought work was your jam. The whole time I've been here you've being going on about work as though your life depended on it or something."

"I lost the Brower and Port deal."

"On account of me?" Ivy asked, her eyes bulging with worry.

"What do *you* think?" Holly snarled. Well, she *would* have snarled had she not been too emotionally exhausted for things like inflection.

"How did I..."

"Ever since you got here, I've been trying to keep you out of trouble," Holly pounced. "As it happens, doing so is a full-time job which makes it basically impossible to hold down a job with any level of responsibility. Compounded by the fact that I'm trying to salvage my relationship with Cash which you severely compromised..."

"Hey man," Ivy perked up. "Don't worry about Brower and Port. They sound like dicks. You'll get 'em next time."

"No," Holly said wearily.

"That doesn't sound like a word you would normally say," Ivy observed. "Unless of course you happen to be talking to me right before I do something dumb."

"I was fired."

"Dude..."

"That's it for me," Holly said, throwing her hands in the air. "I've lost everything I've ever cared about. My career. Dreams. Ambitions. Future. Cash..."

"The good news is," Ivy chirped, "we can finally have time to do stuff together!"

"Ivy, I don't WANT to do stuff together!" Holly wailed. "Can't you see I'm in crisis and this is largely your fault?"

"Oh."

"My life was so uncomplicated before you arrived," Holly moaned.

"Really?" Ivy boggled. "'Cuz it kind of seemed that your life was jumbled with so many details and rules, it made me dizzy just trying to remember how everything is supposed to go. For instance, can I eat yogurt on a Tuesday or is that a weekend thing? Do I sit on that chair that's the shape of a boiled egg or is it just for decoration? Why do you have so many different kinds of spoons and what are they all for? Why am I allowed to eat the mold on one kind of cheese but not the other kind? Will you yell at me if I use Monday's bedsheets on Friday? Which toothbrush is technically mine? Do I wear pants when I answer the door or no? Honestly Sis, I don't think I'm the one who complicated your life."

"Ivy, you ruined everything. Own it."

"Do you... hate me?"

"I don't even have the stamina or the willpower to hate you right now."

"Thanks, Holls," Ivy beamed. "That means the world to me. Say! How's about we snuggle on the couch and sing, *"Chestnuts Roasting on a Garbage Fire?"*

"That's not how that goes."

"That's how it goes in my neighborhood."

"I need to go to bed. For a year."

Ivy blinked and crunched into a burnt angel cookie as Holly shuffled into her bedroom.

CHAPTER TWENTY
(TWO DAYS BEFORE CHRISTMAS)

"I wanna' return this here dress," Ivy said to a prim sales clerk as she scrunched the once-dazzling gown into a ball on the cash counter.

"Inside out?" the clerk said, quirking an eyebrow. "With a mysterious stain on the crotch?"

"It came that way," Ivy said quickly. "I lost the receipt, so you don't have to give me no money back. I'd also like to return these other things in my duffel bag. Nothing fits so..."

"Miss, are these items stolen?"

"Stolen?" Ivy laughed. "Gee, that's cute. Nah. If I stole this stuff it wouldn't make sense for me to be returning everything. That would be zany."

"I think you should leave," the clerk said sternly.

"Okie doke," Ivy shrugged. "Thanks for being so nice about it. Usually when I get kicked out of places there's more yelling and salty language. You're nice."

"Out."

"I like your hair scrunchie."

"You are not welcome back."

"Alrighty!" Ivy waved as she left the boutique. "Have a good one!"

Ivy was just about to dart away as fast as she possibly could from the boutique when she accidentally rammed into the firm body of an unmistakable man.

"Boof!" Ivy boofed into the man's chest which was at perfect eye level. She got a whiff of frankincense.

"Ivy?"

"Casherson?"

"What are you doing here?"

"Just returning some stuff I couldn't afford," Ivy shrugged. "You?"

Cash ballooned his cheeks with air before exhaling.

"You have suitcases," Ivy stated the obvious.

"I'm heading out a day early," Cash said, running his fingers through his hair stressfully. "I can't stand being here a day longer."

"Oh."

"Are… you sure you don't want to come with me?" Cash coaxed. "To Prague?"

"Hey man, we talked about this before…"

"I know, it's just…"

"I don't want you to go."

"Ivy, this is something I have to do."

"No you don't. Holly…"

"It's nice that you're looking out for your sister, but you have to understand things just aren't going to work out with me and Holly. I can't be with someone whose values don't align with mine."

"Then why do you want me to go to Prague? What do I know about values anyhow? I'm about to pop a bastard of questionable origin. His dad may or may not be some scofflaw I had relations with, in that dark alley behind Twitchy's Vape Shack. Or the guy who gives people fake flu vaccines outa' the back of his van. Or Bart. Bart's weird. Oh, and I enjoy the smell of gasoline fumes."

"You have a pure heart," Cash said softly. "I can see that. And it disturbs me that your sister can't…"

"Cash, you don't understand," Ivy pleaded. "Holly is a mess. She lost her deal with those guys, she lost her job…"

"I'm sorry to hear that but…"

"She won't get out of her stinking bed!" Ivy squeaked, tossing her hands in the air desperately. "I've never seen her like this before! I can't convince her to do nothing. She won't watch that Scrooge movie with all the puppets. She won't check out the Christmas market with me. She won't eat any of my special brownies. She doesn't even feel like telling me that I've disgraced the entire family! I'm worried."

"Please don't put that on me," Cash said, raising a hand. "I supported her the best way I know how while constantly taking a backseat to her career. I don't see how I can fix…"

"She needs you!" Ivy begged. "Can't you see that she's a total dumpster fire when you're not around?"

"Ivy," Cash exhaled. "I hear you. I respect what you're saying. But this is personal. I need some distance. I do wish you would reconsider and come along."

"Cash," Ivy squeaked emotionally, "I woulda' loved to go. I care about you somethin' fierce. I can't help it, but I do..."

Cash took Ivy's trembling hands hopefully into his.

"It's just..." Ivy whimpered, "Holly's my sister. She's so good to me, Cash. I don't even deserve all she's done..."

"You do though."

"Cash, no. It was selfish of me to show up, expecting food and free digs."

"You had nowhere to go."

"Only because I made bad choices. Holly was dealt the same deck as me and she built a real career, made a nice ivory home for herself and scored a real neat guy. Holly's had it tough, Cash. If you knew all the junk she had to overcome you wouldn't be so quick to turf her. Her life was harsh and I'm probably some kind of wonky trigger that made everything come rushing back. You can't just take off when she needs you the most, you just can't!"

"Ivy..."

"Holly makes me want to be a better person," Ivy said, blinking away tears.

Cash swallowed hard and then hailed a taxi.

"Cash!" Ivy pleaded.

"Please don't make this harder," Cash's voice cracked emotionally as he stepped into the taxi.

"Cash!"

***

Curled into bed, Holly looked, glassy-eyed, out her ceiling to floor bedroom window at the twinkling Christmas lights that adorned the city outside. She wanted to hate Ivy. Why couldn't she hate Ivy? A swirl of emotion nauseated her as she mused on the complexity of her relationship with her sister. She had been fiercely protective of her from the moment she was born in that horrible apartment where the thermostat was stuck at seventeen degrees and the hallways smelled like pee.

Turning her back on Ivy when her little sister was only sixteen was the hardest thing Holly ever had to do. But she saw no other way to move forward with her life and have a fighting chance to chase her dreams. She was desperate for a better life than what her loopy mother and absentee father were able to give her. But how could she do that when every penny she earned was poured into damage control and bail? Holly cried herself to sleep every night for over a year after she disowned Ivy. Her heart felt sick. But she made the cognizant choice to move ahead and pretend that her past could not define her.

Her life was indeed easier without Ivy.

But she would be lying to herself if she denied that she felt a tingling sensation of relief when Ivy showed up at her apartment unexpectedly. She was alive, not sleeping under a bridge and not being exploited by some nefarious creep in the streets. And because of that, Holly's heart felt a little less sick.

The door slammed and Ivy came running in with her eyes filled with tears.

"Ivy?" Holly asked, sitting up in bed.

"I'm so sorry, Holly!" Ivy sobbed.

"What did you do?" Holly asked nervously.

"He went to Prague!"

Holly looked at Ivy inquisitively.

"Cash!" Ivy sniffled. "I wanted to give him to you for Christmas, but I couldn't stop him..."

Holly's heart literally melted like butter in the microwave.

"Oh, Ivy."

"I wanted to make things right," Ivy snuffed. "Honest!"

Holly exhaled a long, sustained breath. "I know you did," she muttered guiltily.

"How come I can't do nothing right?" Ivy squeaked.

Holly took a deep breath. "Sometimes... things are just outside our control."

"I broke your life."

"Well," Holly said, patting the bed next to her, gesturing for Ivy to plop herself down next to her. "I'm the one who built my life out of glass so..."

"I'm really sorry, Holly. For everything."

"Don't worry about it," Holly sighed. "I'll eventually get the smell out of the sheets."

"What I mean is..."

"It's fine."

"But..."

"You're different, Ivy," Holly said, placing a stray piece of Ivy's straggly hair behind her ear. "You've changed. Grown up."

Ivy lowered her head.

"I can't remember Christmas without Cash," Holly said somberly.

Ivy was about to say something but stopped herself.

***

"Yep," said an airport ticket clerk as she clacked the keys of her computer, lolling her eyes up and down the screen. "We do have a flight to Prague departing later this evening, with a layover in Minsk."

"Minsk?" Cash said, crinkling his nose. "That's nowhere near Prague."

"If that doesn't suit you, I could fly you out on boxing day."

"Fine," Cash exhaled. "Book me."

"It'll be an upgrade," the clerk said, still clacking. "You'll need to pay an additional three hundred and seventy-five dollars."

Burbling his lips with defeat, Cash reached for his wallet, patting around his back pocket. "What the…"

"Something wrong, Dr. Bartholomew?" the clerk said blandly, not averting her eyes from the screen.

"I can't find my wallet," Cash said, instantly reddening.

The ticket clerk crossed her arms.

"I must have set it down somewhere," Cash apologized. "I'll be… I'll be right back." Cash winced at the long lineup of people behind him and sliced through the crowd of irritated travelers.

CHAPTER TWENTY-ONE
(CHRISTMAS EVE)

While sleeping alongside Holly in her bed, Ivy lay sprawled in a mess of tangled sheets, while Holly was wrapped perfectly into a blankety cocoon. Lying flumped on the floor was Ivy's duffel bag, partially unzipped with a hint of Cash's wallet peeping out. Holly's phone vibrated next to her bed with Cash's name on the call display, but Holly could not be awoken from her emotional coma.

A few moments later, Ivy awoke suddenly with her eyes popping open like those of a child.

"Hey! Holly!" Ivy squealed, scrambling in her sheets. "It's today!"

"Thanks for that," Holly moaned dozily.

"It's our first Christmas together," Ivy said, unravelling Holly from her cocoon, "in seven years!"

"Christmas isn't until tomorrow," Holly moaned, pulling a pillow over her head.

"In Germany they do Christmas a day early," Ivy quipped. "Let's be Germans!"

"Wake me in January," Holly muffled from under the pillow. "We can be Ukrainians."

Totally ignoring Holly, Ivy coaxed her out of bed. "Close your eyes."

"They are closed," Holly grunted.

"Keep them closed," Ivy said, leading Holly into the living room.

"What's all this about?"

"Okay, open!"

When Holly opened her eyes, she blinked a few times at her perfectly fake, ivory Christmas tree. Not a single ornament out of place.

"Are you surprised?" Ivy beamed.

"My tree?" Holly blinked. "Where's the Broomers' tree?"

"I returned it to the Broomers."

"How?"

"Same way I took it out."

"I don't even want to know."

"See?" Ivy squealed, practically jumping. "I decorated it exactly the way you like it. I did it while you were asleep. Took me practically all night."

Holly goggled when she spotted presents under the tree, wrapped sloppily.

"Oh, Ivy. Presents?"

"You gotta' have something to open on Christmas Day!" Ivy chimed. "Or today if you want to be Germans."

"With Mom's reputation, who's to say we're not German?" Holly said, opening a closet and revealing hidden presents which she lugged over to the tree. "Or Greek. Korean. Maltese. Lithuanian…"

With childlike enthusiasm, Ivy tore open a present. Inside the parcel she found a breast pump.

"Yes!" Ivy cheered. "A jar with a funnel on it! This is awesome! I can think of like eleven different things I can do with this thing! No wait. Twelve!"

"Honey, no. It's a breast pump. For the baby."

"Oh," Ivy said quizzically, eyeballing the contraption.

"Can I open one?" Holly wondered tentatively.

Ivy nodded vigorously.

Demurely undoing the tape on her present, Holly discovered a very familiar painting underneath the reused wrapping paper. Looking up at the wall, Holly noticed that a piece of artwork was missing. After a brief pause, Holly burst into uncontrollable laughter.

"Do you like it?" Ivy asked tentatively.

"Of course I like it," Holly laughed. "I bought it myself three years ago! What's that one?" Holly teased, pointing to another unopened present. "Did you wrap up my bohemian crystal candle sticks?"

"No," Ivy said sheepishly. "It's your salad spinner."

Holly laughed harder.

"Dude," Ivy tried to explain, reddening, "I couldn't afford to buy you nothing. I got some stuff from one of them snooty boutiques you like but I took them back 'cuz…"

"Hun," Holly chuckled, not noticing her cell phone vibrating, "it is totally okay. You know what we should do? Let's have cookies for breakfast and share a bowl of honey roasted nuts."

"Like at the Spencers' on Christmas morning!"

"I'll put on the kettle," Holly announced as she stood to her feet.

Holly stopped in her tracks when there was a knock at the door.

"Maybe it's Cash!" Ivy said hopefully.

When Holly opened the door, there stood two police officers waiting in the hall.

"Officers?" Holly said, stunned.

Ivy froze with terror.

"Sorry to bother you during the holidays," an officer said. "We're looking for someone."

Ivy frantically looked around the room for a means of escape.

"Oh my God," Holly said, paling. "Is everything okay?"

The second officer offered Holly a picture of Ivy. "Have you seen this woman?" he asked. "Ivy Plover?"

Utterly stunned, Holly's jaw dropped. "I... she's... why do you ask?"

"She escaped from prison three months ago," the first officer responded.

"Prison?" Holly gasped. "What did she do?"

"Why? Do you know her?"

"Uh..."

"There she is," the second officer said, pointing to Ivy who was pathetically trying to hide behind the Christmas tree.

Before Holly could do or say anything, the officers seized Ivy who was oddly compliant and seemingly unsurprised.

"Ivy?" Holly squeaked.

Ivy merely looked at Holly imploringly.

"I don't understand," Holly said. "What's going on here?"

"It was good of you to leave us a trail of stolen credit card purchases," the second officer said while handcuffing Ivy. "Thanks for that."

With her mind still whirring with confusion, Holly spun around and discovered the first officer emerging from the bedroom with Cash's wallet.

"Cash Bartholomew," the officer stated. "This belong to anyone here or shall I report it as stolen?"

"How did you get Cash's wallet?" Holly whisper-shrieked to Ivy.

"I swear I was trying to help," Ivy said tearfully. "I couldn't stop him from leaving you. I thought if I took his wallet..."

"Don't go anywhere," the first officer said to Holly as they took Ivy away. "We'll be sending someone over to question you."

"Don't get Holly in trouble," Ivy implored. "She didn't know."

"Officers, wait!" Holly quavered. "You can't take her to prison. She's pregnant."

Ivy's face wrenched into a state of agony and contrition.

"Ivy," Holly begged, "tell them about the baby."

"I'm so sorry," Ivy sobbingly implored.

"You lied?"

"I wanted to stay," Ivy wept. "I feel so bad. You have to believe me."

"Come on, Fingers," the first officer said, tugging Ivy out of the room.

"Holly, please listen!" Ivy shrieked from the hallway.

Holly turned her face away and said, "I am such an idiot."

"No, Holly! You're not!" Ivy could be heard screaming from down the hall. "Holly?"

Holly closed the door and put her face in her hands.

CHAPTER TWENTY-TWO

Bedraggled from lack of sleep, Cash was awakened from his slumber on an uncomfortable airport terminal chair when his cell phone rang. Nursing a kink in his neck, he answered groggily. "Holly? For God's sake, I've left like eighteen messages. Why haven't you been answering the... Ivy?"

"I gotta' make this quick," Ivy said on a cell phone from prison. "They're coming for me in a few."

"Where are you?" Cash said dozily while rubbing his neck tendons.

"Prison," Ivy said matter-of-factly. "Where are you?"

"Prison?" Cash said, suddenly jolting awake. "Ivy, what's happening? Where's Holly? Why do you have Holly's phone? Why are you in prison?"

"Whoa," Ivy said, shaking the confusion from her head, "give me a minute to process all that. Okay. I just got in my orange jumpsuit and now I'm waiting to get yelled at, I assume Holly's still at home, I stole her phone and I'm a criminal. Did I miss anything?"

"This is unreal," Cash said, rubbing his eyes. "Ivy, are you okay?"

"Yeah," Ivy nodded, "I'm okay. This prison stuff is old hat. But this call isn't about me. You got Holly all wrong. She didn't really lie to you. It's just, our life was real sad. It ain't fair to smack a guy in the face with your lousy childhood. Not the guy you're ape over."

"Ivy…"

"I ain't finished," Ivy interrupted. "Holly didn't have to take me in, you know. How often do you wreck a person's life and then get a second chance? You shoulda' seen how good Holly took care of me when she thought I was pregnant. She gave me vitamins, presents, rules, a funnel…"

"Wait a minute, what?" Cash said, squinting with bewilderment. "Since when were you *not* having a baby?"

"I'd explain but neither of us have that kind of time," Ivy said, eyeballing the room for guards. "My point being, Holly is perfect. Warts and all. Letting her go is the biggest mistake you'll ever make. Trust me. If mistake-makin' was an art form, I'd be frickin' Picasso. I'm here to tell ya, one goof can turn your whole world upside-down."

"It's more complicated than that," Cash sighed.

"Is it?" Ivy quipped. "Then why are there eighteen messages on Holly's phone right now?"

"I…" Cash stammered. "…didn't know who else to call."

Some officers entered the room, causing Ivy to scramble.

"Gotta' go," Ivy said quickly.

"Wait, Ivy…"

Cash ended the call and exhaled.

***

Musing regretfully, Ivy sat alone, slumped in her prison cell. A large, bushy-eyebrowed woman, built like an intimidating, rocky crag grumbled in the cell next to hers.

"Christmas is just like any other day, Sister," Scary Maud rumbled. "Just another etch on the wall."

"Shut up, Scary Maud," Ivy said woefully.

"Nobody gives a flying squirrel about you," Scary Maud continued to taunt. "Not this day or any other. Are you going to finish your mashed potatoes?"

Ivy apathetically took a handful of lumpy mashed potatoes from her tray of pathetic, uneaten food, balled it up and hurled it at Scary Maud through the bars.

***

"This way," a prison guard said to Holly as they walked through a stark, prison hallway.

Very self-conscious and trying to walk with confidence, Holly walked primly down the hall with a bag of take-out food. She tried not to wince as intimidating women caterwauled at Holly from their cells. The guard who accompanied her lead Holly around the corner.

***

Holly's apartment was empty when there was a knock at the door. When nobody answered, the knocker knocked again.

"Holly?" Cash called as he let himself in.

Cash scanned the room, but he was alone.

***

When the guard led Holly to Ivy's cell, Holly noticed Ivy lying limply on her cot with a tear rolling down her cheek. Holly stared at her sister for a moment. Ivy was looking so small and vulnerable.

"You have one hour," the guard instructed Holly.

Holly nodded and then focused again on her little sister.

"You could have at least put up some garland," Holly said, breaking the silence.

"Seriously?" Ivy chimed, instantly leaping to her feet with excitement.

"On my list of things I enjoy doing alone," Holly said, bursting the staples on the paper take-out bag, "Christmas is the very last."

"What did you bring?" Ivy beamed, wiping a residual tear away. "Something better than modified turkey and rubber gravy, I hope. Prison food is narsty."

"I figured," Holly said, passing some chopsticks to Ivy through the bars, "since you're not actually pregnant, there's no reason we can't eat raw fish."

"See?" Ivy said to Scary Maud, jerking her head in the direction of her basically perfect sister. "My sister brought yuppy food. Jealous much?"

Scary Maud snarled in her cell.

"I thought this is a women's prison," Holly whispered, leaning in confidentially.

"We're almost sure Scary Maud is a woman," Ivy whispered back. "Nobody wants to check."

"Hey!" Scary Maud barked from her cell. "What are the two of you clucking about? Don't make me thump you!"

"Go cork yourself!" Ivy squawked back. Then she turned to Holly and said giddily, "I can't believe you're here!"

"As it turns out," Holly said with her mouth full of eel, "I want to be here. And so does someone else."

Holly released Poindexter from her purse.

"Pointexter!" Ivy jubilantly squealed.

"Hey!" barked Scary Maud. "No squirrels in the can!"

"Shut your gob, Shrew!" Ivy shrieked. Then turning back to Holly she asked, "Are you sure you're okay spending Christmas in the clink?"

"Anything's better than an empty apartment," Holly shrugged.

***

Cash pulled a steaming turkey out of Holly's oven and placed it on her dining room table which he had romantically set for two. After taking a deep breath and looking at his watch, Cash sat at the table. He looked longingly at the empty seat beside him, then glanced at the door.

***

Holly hugged Ivy through the prison bars.

"You should know," Ivy said, clinging tightly to Holly so she would not let go, "when I showed up that night, I was hidin' from the cops. Tryin' to take advantage."

"I know," Holly said.

"But after," Ivy sniffled, "when we was havin' Christmas together like real sisters? I tried so hard to undo it all. To fix things. You made me want to be a good person. Like you."

"I know that too," Holly coughed emotionally.

"What happens next?" Ivy asked, retracting from the hug.

"We'll see how it goes," Holly said, squeezing Ivy's hand through the bars.

CHAPTER TWENTY-THREE

Cash adjusted and preened himself when he heard Holly opening the door. Holly was agog when she discovered Cash waiting for her with a romantic, Christmas dinner.

"Cash," Holly said, stunned.

"I forgot to give back my key," Cash said, nervously fidgeting.

They stared at each other, mystified for a moment.

"I tried calling…" Cash began.

"I lost my phone."

Cash smirked and nodded.

"Ivy mentioned Prague," Holly said after an awkward beat of silence.

"Yeah, I didn't get very far."

"Shame."

"My wallet went missing. I couldn't upgrade so I stayed overnight at the airport to take my original flight out on Christmas Eve. I tried calling you to see if you could spot me some money… maybe meet up at the…"

Another awkward pause.

"Why are you here?" Holly finally asked.

"I bumped into someone en route," Cash replied. "A mad prophet of sorts."

"Really."

"She told me that one goof could turn your entire world upside-down."

"Wise."

Yet another awkward pause.

"Why didn't you tell me?" Cash blurted. "About... you know. Everything."

"It's embarrassing," Holly said, pinkening like undercooked turkey.

"Why? None of it was your fault. You were just a little girl."

"I wanted to be with you more than anything. What would you have thought of me?"

"Give me some credit."

"You have no idea the prejudice I had to overcome," Holly insisted. "All the stigmas."

"Of course I had no idea. Because you never told me."

"How could I? Look at you, Cash. You're flawless."

"In what reality am I flawless?" Cash squeaked with laughter. "I was orphaned at six and raised by a zany aunt who tried to pay for groceries with buttons. I snore. I'm afraid of spiders. You're always complaining that I smell like asparagus. And the subject of which I have the firmest grasp? Feet."

Holly stifled laughter.

"Feet!" Cash repeated for dramatic effect. "I love them. Feet are my life. I could talk about them all day. Is that cool? Is that virile? Hell no. I could have been a steamy brain surgeon. A hipster cardiologist. An alluring pediatrician. But no. I'm a foot nerd. The least cool doctor in the medical field. Second least if you count proctologists."

Holly snorted with laughter.

"Holly, you only think I'm perfect because I'm perfect for you."

Cash pulled out a chair, inviting Holly to sit. "Turkey?" he inquired.

"I already ate," Holly apologized sheepishly.

"Oh," Cash said, sagging with disappointment. "That's unfortunate. I put something special in the stuffing."

"Sorry. Ivy and I had sushi in prison. I..." Holly paused when she saw Cash smirking. "Wait... Something special is in the stuffing? How special?"

Cash shrugged mischievously.

"I could eat," Holly said, sitting down with her eyes bulging.

Cash smiled as he sat down to eat with Holly. Holly reached for a bowl of stuffing, but Cash beat her to it. Waiting for the stuffing, Holly nearly burst with anxiousness.

"Pass the stuffing?" Holly said, bouncing in her seat with anticipation.

"In a minute," Cash teased.

Cash took his time dishing stuffing onto his plate, enjoying Holly's restless leg syndrome. Once he passed the stuffing to Holly, she put several heaping scoops on her plate as though she was looking for something.

"You seem awfully hungry for someone who just ate," Cash jibed.

"Screw this," Holly said, giving up on the serving spoon and digging through the stuffing with her hands.

Cash laughed wildly at Holly who was making a colossal, buttery mess. Once the bowl was empty, Holly frantically broke apart clumps of stuffing, looking for something.

"Stupid stuffing," Holly cussed, flinging gummy onions from her fingernails.

Cash discreetly took an engagement ring out of the cavity of the turkey carcass.

"Looking for this?" Cash asked coyly.

Holly stopped abruptly, covered in sage and mushy stuffing and looking very unladylike. After a stunned moment, Holly impulsively jumped Cash and kissed him passionately.

"I should have used more sage," Cash said after licking his lips.

"Oh my God," Holly said, suddenly realizing how utterly covered in stuffing she was. "I look revolting! Give me ten minutes to shower. We'll rewind this whole thing and do it officially once I fix myself up. Do that thing with the ring again... I just got this cute fuzzy sweater... and my hair... everything's going to be perf..."

"This is the hottest you've ever looked," Cash said, fluttering his eyelids desirously before kissing Holly again.

Their awkwardly long kiss was suddenly interrupted by a knock at the door. Holly and Cash looked at each other, perplexed.

"You expecting someone?" Cash asked with a quirked eyebrow.

Holly answered the door and found a seedy looking young lady with a tattered pageboy hat, goggling at Holly expectantly.

"Hey," the strange girl said familiarly.

Holly and Cash blinked.

"I'm Carol."

Awkward pause.

"Holly's sister," the girl explained.

Cash looked inquisitively at Holly, cocking his head.

"I only have one sister, I swear to God," Holly insisted.

"Yeah," Carol said, scuffing her shoe against the carpet. "Mom got around." Carol sniffed the air. "Hey, is that turkey?"

Holly and Cash gaped.

www.ingramcontent.com/pod-product-compliance
Lightning Source LLC
Chambersburg PA
CBHW071518170626
46811CB00007B/2895